THE BARFLY

The last thing the Barfly remembers is leading a raid against the Rebels in 1865. But it is now 1872, and he only knows that he had come to Redrock disguised as a drunk called the Barfly. He finds work on a homestead, and when it is attacked by mysterious cattle rustlers, even the Barfly is amazed at how fast he is with a six-gun. At last, his memory begins to return. Now he must confront the past. Was he hero or villain? Only time — and hot lead — would tell!

Books by Edwin Derek
in the Linford Western Library:

ROWDY'S RAIDERS
ROWDY'S RETURN

EDWIN DEREK

THE BARFLY

Complete and Unabridged

LINFORD
Leicester

First published in Great Britain in 2001 by
Robert Hale Limited
London

First Linford Edition
published 2003
by arrangement with
Robert Hale Limited
London

British Library CIP Data

Derek, Edwin
    The barfly.—Large print ed.—
Linford western library
1. Western stories
2. Large type books
I. Title
823.9′14 [F]

ISBN 0–7089–4918–5

Published by
F. A. Thorpe (Publishing)
Anstey, Leicestershire

Set by Words & Graphics Ltd.
Anstey, Leicestershire
Printed and bound in Great Britain by
T. J. International Ltd., Padstow, Cornwall

This book is printed on acid-free paper

1

Slowly the buzzing sound filling his head began to die away. It seemed to have been there for ever. The fog he had lived in for as long as he could remember rolled back. This had happened before, but each time he had stepped back into it, retreating into the mind-numbing safety of oblivion.

Not this time. Like a dog shaking itself after a long swim, he shook the last of the fog away. With it went the last remnants of the noise in his head. Finally, full unimpaired consciousness returned. It had been a long time coming. With it came the vivid memory of a cavalry charge; a violent explosion, then nothing but the fog. No! he was not going back into that again, but where were his men? Someone yelling loudly brought him back into the real world.

'Hey, Barfly. I don't pay you to stand around dreaming. Get this place swept out and empty the spittoons. Jump to it, the boss will be here soon and you know he can't bear to have you in the bar once it's open. He says your stench drives away the customers. It's pay day, so you can drink yourself stupid again, so long as it's not in here. But no work, no pay. Understand?'

There was a broom in his hand and the bartender was yelling at him. He shook his head. He was in a saloon, but he had no idea how he had got there, what day it was, or even which year.

He looked up at the big mirror but barely recognized his own reflection. His large brown beard was stained with food, his hair looked as if it had not been washed for months and the state of his clothes defied description. So while he tried to figure things out, he began to sweep. Only then did he begin to notice the vile smell. It was an almost indescribable mixture of urine, vomit and something else he would rather not think about.

It took an hour to finish the job to the satisfaction of the bartender. The big clock behind the bar registered a little after noon. He left the saloon and automatically headed down the street, yet the vile smell stayed with him. He was shocked to discover it came from him.

People in the street looked contemptuously at him, or gave him a wide berth. However, he did not recognize any of them, nor could he remember anything about the town he now found himself in. Yet, automatically, he crossed the street and walked into the livery stable. Somehow it seemed familiar.

The livery stable also doubled as the blacksmith's. A big forge smouldered in the corner, but the place was deserted except for an old black gig which appeared to have been recently repaired. Were its owner and the blacksmith having lunch together, possibly haggling over the price of the repair?

Whatever they were doing, he was alone. He hurried across the stable yard into a small paddock. Somehow he knew there would be a water-trough big enough to bathe in.

By the trough was a black iron hand-pump. He used it to fill up the trough, then dived in, boots, clothes and all. The clear, cold water splashed over the sides of the trough, forming muddy pools on the sunbaked ground. He ducked under the water again and again until the worst of the dirt and smell disappeared.

He had just finished bathing when he heard a woman screaming. Still dripping water, he squelched into the stable. Pinned against the side of the gig was a woman. Her long black hair swung to and fro as she tried to fight off her huge assailant.

Although from his appearance the giant was obviously the blacksmith, the Barfly did not recognize him. Nor had he any recollection of ever seeing the woman. She fought hard, but stood no chance against the huge blacksmith. The giant's massive hand tore the shoulder of her blouse, exposing most of the woman's well-formed breasts.

She screamed but the huge blacksmith only laughed. So she raked the fingernails of her right hand across his face, causing his laughter to change to a howl of pain. He struck the woman viciously with the open palm of his hand, sending her sprawling.

Water still streaming from his ragged clothes, the Barfly stepped between the giant and the prostrate woman. Sure that this was not just a lover's tiff, he was not about to stand by and let the blacksmith rape her, whoever she was.

'That's quite enough of that,' he said firmly.

Both the blacksmith and the woman had been so preoccupied with their struggle that neither had noticed the arrival of the Barfly. However, far from being annoyed by the interruption, the giant blacksmith roared with laughter. He treated the Barfly with contempt and went to brush his would-be opponent aside. His first shock came as his crude swing was skilfully avoided by his much smaller opponent.

Without a word, the Barfly counter-attacked. Diving to his right, he hit the ground, rolled forward and tripped the giant.

Taken by surprise, the blacksmith crashed backwards to the ground. Before he could recover the Barfly rolled over on to his back, swung his legs across the supine man, then brought the heel of his old cavalry boot sharply down on the giant's nose. The blacksmith roared out in agony, then choked as his blood gushed into his open mouth.

The Barfly gave him no chance to recover. He could not afford to give the blacksmith, who outweighed him by nearly seventy pounds, any chance at all. While the giant was still choking on the ground, the Barfly jumped up and drove his foot viciously into the temple of his prostrate foe. The giant was instantly knocked unconscious.

Once again the Barfly was filthy. His wet clothes were covered with the dirt from the stable floor. To make matters worse, he had rolled over some horse dung during the fight. Not that the woman was in much better condition. Her white blouse had been torn to shreds and her cream, ankle-length skirt was covered in filth.

'Into the gig,' she gasped. 'We must get away before Brad's cronies come to see what happened.'

The Barfly started to say an officer of the Union Cavalry ran from nobody, but the woman cut him short. For some reason, she seemed angry at him.

'Explanations later, I don't want anyone to see me in this state,' she said tersely, as she pointed at her half-naked breasts.

Even so, she drove the gig out of town slowly. When he asked why, her response was equally abrupt.

'To avoid attracting attention.'

The Barfly could only wonder at her

composure after her ordeal. As they left town, they passed by a sign on which was written WELCOME TO REDROCK. However, the name meant nothing to him.

Only when Redrock was well behind them did the woman increase speed to a gallop. It was not long before the little pony began to blow hard. However, they did not slow down until she turned off the main trail and headed towards her homestead. In spite of the state of her blouse, she made no attempt to cover her breasts, seemingly more concerned about the possibility of pursuit than her modesty.

Apart from considering himself to be too much of a gentleman to take full advantage of the woman's situation, the Barfly had other things on his mind. Like the town, the countryside was completely unfamiliar to him. In fact he was sure he had never seen it before. What was left of his memory was so fragmented it was no use. Worse still, he could not even remember his name.

It was almost dusk when they reached the homestead. During the trip the woman said little, although she kept looking behind her as if fearing they would be overtaken. However, her fears proved to be groundless.

The Barfly unhitched the pony and led it into the paddock by the house. He used some cloth out of the gig to give the sweating and exhausted beast a thorough rub down. The job took well over an hour and it was dark by the time he had finished.

The house was much bigger and better-appointed than the usual homestead. He entered through a small porch and walked into the main living room. In front of a large roaring fire was a tin bath full of steaming hot water. A door at the back of the living room led to the kitchen, from which came the delightful smell of supper cooking.

'No food until you have had a bath. It will take me long enough to get rid of the smell as it is,' shouted the woman from the kitchen.

Though he was by no means a big man, he had to crouch almost double to get into the bath, which was just as well for his modesty, as she entered the room as soon as he had manoeuvred himself into the tin bath. She had changed into a blue gingham dress, but her long black hair was still dishevelled.

She smiled as he blushed, then picked up his evil-smelling clothes and left the room. He had only just breathed a sigh of relief when she returned carrying a wooden tray on which was a large bar of carbolic soap, a cut-throat razor and a pair of scissors.

Ignoring his cries of protest and taking full advantage of his embarrassment, she set to work on him. She washed and cut his hair, then shaved off his beard. Finally she scrubbed his back, neck and shoulders with the carbolic soap until they were sore. She did not stop until he was spotlessly clean. However, she took pity on his panic when she started to wash his loins.

'Such a fuss about a little thing,' she said, but she was laughing as she returned to the kitchen.

A few minutes later she shouted that she was about to serve dinner. Although it smelled good, he hesitated. She had taken his old clothes. Little better than rags and disgustingly smelly, they were still better than nothing. He was not going to walk naked into the kitchen.

As if she had read his thoughts, she opened the kitchen door and threw in a very large and feminine pink towel. He got out of the tub, dried himself, then wrapped the towel tightly around him. Gingerly he entered the kitchen, only marginally less embarrassed than when she had seen him naked in the bath. The fact that the pink towel was covered in a highly female perfume did nothing to lessen his embarrassment.

Seeing the expression on his face she burst out laughing. In spite of his predicament, he could not but notice she <u>was</u> stunningly beautiful. She looked to be in her mid-twenties and was well above average height. Her firm breasts stood out under her gingham dress, the tightness of which only served to emphasize the slender nature of her figure. The paleness of her skin contrasted with her long, raven-coloured hair. Yet it was the hint of sadness in her eyes which caught his attention.

As he had already experienced when she scrubbed his back, her hands were very soft, suggesting she was not used to the range, or hard work. However, she gave little away about herself as they ate the stew she had prepared.

As for himself, how could he tell her he could not remember his own name, or where he was, or even what year it was? So they sat in silence, except for when she laughed at his embarrassment as he reached for the salt, causing his towel to slip to the floor.

The house contained two bedrooms. Although it was still early evening, the woman led him to the smaller one and left him there. He climbed slowly into the double bed that almost filled the room and was asleep in an instant.

He slept like a log all night, so he neither heard nor felt the woman as she came into the room. She carried a pile of clothes which she dropped at the foot of the bed. She wore only the flimsiest of nightgowns, yet sat on the bed and stroked his forehead gently. Realizing he was sound asleep she sighed sadly and left the room without disturbing him.

It was long past dawn when the Barfly finally awoke. At first the surroundings confused him, then the memory of the previous day came flooding back. But nothing more than the previous day; before that there was a virtual blank, and still he could not remember his name.

He found the clothes at the foot of the bed. To his surprise they fitted him perfectly, yet it felt as if something was missing as he walked into the kitchen.

The woman again wore the blue gingham dress. However, her jet-black hair had been brushed back neatly into place. It was as if yesterday had never happened.

She smiled as she saw that he was dressed in the clothes she had left in the bedroom. The Barfly was overwhelmed by her beauty. The warmth of her smile made him feel good, something he had not felt for a very long time. So, over breakfast he began to explain his loss of memory.

'So, if you didn't know who I was, why did you help me? You took a terrible risk, didn't you? Nobody fights Brad.'

'No, there wasn't any risk. I never had any doubt that I could beat the blacksmith. I didn't have to think about it, everything seemed to come naturally to me. It's sort of weird, not knowing what you are or what you can do.'

For a moment, a look of deep sadness marred her natural beauty. She seemed to be about to say something,

14

then stopped. She paused for a moment, then started again. The Barfly had no way of knowing she had decided not to tell him what she knew about his past. Instead, she introduced herself.

'Well, let's start from the beginning. I'm Mary Foster. I'm a widow. My husband was killed just before the war ended.'

'I'm sorry to hear that, Mrs Foster.'

'It seems a long time ago, but do call me Mary. What shall I call you? Barfly seems so degrading. Do you remember why you did such menial work? After all you proved that you could take care of yourself yesterday, yet you let the whole town continually insult and abuse you.'

'I'm sorry, but I've no idea. It was like waking up with a terrible hangover, but instead of not being able to remember a few hours, I can't remember anything except . . .'

'Except what?' Mary encouraged him gently.

'I remember leading my men in a charge. There was an explosion, then

15

nothing. I say 'my' men, but I can only remember them vaguely.'

'Shut your eyes. Can you try to picture them following you?'

'Yes,' he replied, his voice betraying the anguish he felt.

'Can you see how many men you commanded and the colour of their uniform?'

Sweat began to pour from his brow. For several moments he did not reply, then his hands began to shake. He seemed to be going through some private hell. She was about to tell him to stop when he answered.

'I remember! It was a sunny morning and there were about a dozen men riding behind me. They wore blue tunics.'

'Cavalry men?' Mary asked.

'Yes.' His voice was barely audible.

'That's enough,' said Mary firmly. 'I don't want you to turn back into a bar-bum. Anyway, you haven't finished your breakfast; don't let good food go to waste.'

Gratefully he opened his eyes. He was glad to give up, for the effort of remembering brought back the dark fog. However, as long as he could hear Mary's voice there was no danger of his taking the route to oblivion again. Just for a brief moment her last words struck a distant chord, then it was gone again as she continued.

'Does the name Harry mean anything to you?'

'No, should it?'

Her answer was cut short by the sound of approaching horses. Without knowing why, the Barfly knew the riders would not be friendly towards him, although Mary would be in little danger from them unless they found him.

'Do you have any handguns in the house?' he asked, keeping his voice as calm as he could.

She did not answer, but rushed to her bedroom and returned almost immediately, carrying a holster and a small box of ammunition. In the holster was a superb Navy Colt, so called because of the naval scene depicted on its butt, not because of any special maritime association. All Navy Colts fired .38 calibre bullets which had to be made up by the user. The Navy Colt was a fine handgun, although far less popular than the larger .44 calibre Army Colt.

While the Barfly buckled on the handgun, Mary opened the door to find six riders, including the sheriff, waiting for her. Sheriff Ben Webster was a pleasant enough man in his fifties, but no great shakes as a law-enforcement officer. However, he was basically an honest man.

His deputy, Zack Blake, was another matter altogether. Since the end of the Civil War he had hired out his gun to the highest bidder. It was rumoured he had outdrawn seven men and killed more in cold blood. These rumours Zack Blake did little to dispel. Indeed, he seemed to revel in the notoriety.

'A little off your beaten track aren't you, Sheriff Webster? Won't you and your boys stop and have a bite to eat?' said Mary, although she did not really want them to go into the house and discover the Barfly.

'Got a few questions for you,' interrupted Zack Blake. 'Where's your old gig?'

'Round the back in the paddock where I always keep it when I'm not using it,' replied Mary quite truthfully.

'Mary, would you mind telling me when you picked it up from the livery stable?' asked the sheriff.

'About noon yesterday. I collected it from the blacksmith, then came straight home.'

'Did you see anyone other than Brad?' asked the sheriff.

'Only the Barfly,' replied Mary, again quite truthfully. 'What's this all about?'

'Brad got himself beaten up pretty badly some time yesterday afternoon. There's quite a lot of money missing and the Barfly ain't nowhere to be found,' said Zack Blake.

'You're surely not suggesting the

Barfly was responsible? In his condition he couldn't hurt a fly; besides, he hasn't the brains left to plan a robbery.'

'I think you're right Mary,' said Sheriff Webster. 'Yet it's strange he disappeared about the same time the robbery happened.'

'I think he was part of a gang sent to spy on the town. No one is that stupid,' said Zack. 'If I see him I'll shoot first, ask questions later.'

It was on the tip of Mary's tongue to say that that was the way Zack normally acted, but this was not the time to get into an argument with the trigger-happy deputy. Every moment he remained increased the chances of him dismounting and searching the house. Fortunately Sheriff Webster seemed to have other ideas.

'We must be getting on,' he said. 'Take care, Mary, there may be a gang on the loose. I don't like to think of you out here on your own. You ought to get yourself a handyman you can trust.'

'If not I could come and keep an eye

on you,' called Zack, as they rode away.

That was the last thing Mary wanted. She saw the way Zack looked at her, undressing her with his cold grey eyes. Yet there was no lust in them, just something almost unnatural. It was not just thoughts of her ordeal with the blacksmith which made her shiver, as she walked back into the house.

However, the sheriff had given her an idea which might keep Zack away, if only the Barfly would agree to it. She need not have worried, for he consented without a moment's hesitation.

2

Two days later the stage stopped at Mary's homestead. It had diverted from its normal route, partly to deliver mail and partly at the sheriff's request. Whatever else Ben Webster's failings were as a law-enforcement officer, he did his best to keep a check on Mary's safety.

The Barfly met the stage, collected the mail and began to talk to the driver. It was to be the first test of Mary's handiwork. Under his new white Stetson his hair was considerably lighter than nature had intended, yet it was made to look natural by the pallor of his recently shaved skin.

Mary had found him a pair of expensive Texas-style cowboy boots to replace his old ones. As the Barfly he had worn a pair of old cavalry boots. They had a distinctive pattern on their sides which would have given him away immediately. Surprisingly the new boots, like the hat and new clothes, fitted him perfectly. He guessed they, and the Navy Colt, now slung low from his right hip, had originally belonged to Mary's late husband. However, he thought it better not to ask in case the subject distressed her.

He looked nothing like the filthy creature the townsfolk had called the Barfly. So it was not so surprising that the stage-driver failed to recognize him as he introduced himself as Harry Brown.

His story was his horse had broken its leg in a nearby gopher hole, so he had been forced to shoot it, after which he had walked to the nearest house for help. Finding its owner needed someone to help out, he agreed to work for her until he had earned enough money to buy another horse.

A mustang or pony cost about thirty dollars, but a good horse would cost four or five times as much. A cowboy's wage was set by the powerful Cattle-men's Association at thirty dollars a month, or a dollar a day. This low rate of pay gave the Barfly, masquerading as Harry Brown, a good excuse to stay with Mary for a few months. For very different reasons they both hoped his memory would return before then.

It had taken Mary and him most of yesterday to come up with the story, which the driver readily accepted as they hoped he would. In 1868 there were few railroads in the West and fewer telegraph lines. As a result stagecoach drivers were considered to be a good source of news. The driver's return to Redrock would see the story of the arrival of a stranger at the Foster homestead spread all over the town. From the description the driver would almost certainly give of Mary Foster's new hired help they hoped nobody would link him to the Barfly.

They had chosen his new name carefully. For some reason Mary insisted on calling him Harry. After much discussion they decided Brown was the sort of common name which might have been real or an alias. They decided to give their creation a hint of mystery to make him more believable.

After the stage had left, Harry, as he now thought of himself, decided to have a look around the homestead. He soon discovered that it was considerably larger than the normal eighty acres allocated to settlers. Behind the barn, which was situated at the end of the paddock furthest from the house, he discovered a grave, marked only by a wooden cross which bore no name. If it was Mary's husband, why had she not had his name engraved on a proper tombstone?

The size of the homestead posed a problem. He had neither a horse nor, more important, a saddle. He had no doubt that he could use the gig's pony if only he had a saddle. However, getting one was going to be a problem. Even if he had the money, he could not buy one in Redrock without raising suspicion. Shooting a horse with a broken leg was a plausible story, but no one would believe he had left his saddle on it.

In the West a saddle, together with a hat, which was rarely removed, and boots, were the cowboy's most prized possessions. Whether on the range, or at roundup time, or on the long cattle drives, cowboys spent most of their waking hours in the saddle. As most big ranches provided a remuda of mustangs to ride, it was not unusual to see a sixty-dollar saddle on a thirty-dollar pony. Many cowboys bought even more expensive saddles, even though their wage was hardly enough to support a family. Perhaps that was why most cowboys were young and single.

Suddenly Harry was interrupted by the arrival of two riders. He had been so busy looking round and so engrossed in his thoughts that he had failed to notice them ride up. Raised voices indicated the riders were not friendly, so he hurried back.

The house was between him and the riders, so they failed to see him. He paused in the shadow cast by the house. Perhaps because he moved so quietly, or possibly because they were not expecting to meet anyone else, neither of the riders noticed him.

'I've no intention of selling to anybody,' said Mary angrily. 'As for me not working the land, what does a cowboy know about farming? I've two fields of corn, plus milking-cows, geese and hens. Redrock takes all I can produce, so I manage very nicely, thank you.'

'It's not right that a pretty woman should be on her own so far out of town. Anything might happen,' said one of the riders as he dismounted.

'She's not alone,' said Harry, stepping out of the shadows, hand poised over his newly acquired Navy Colt.

Startled, the dismounted rider swung round to face Harry. He was dressed like an Eastern dude in a red shirt and black breeches. He looked little more than a boy, yet already there were four notches on the pearl butt of his silver-plated six-gun. His right hand moved towards it, but before he could draw, his companion, still mounted, called out to stop him.

'Hold up there, Bill. Remember what the boss said — no trouble until he says so.'

He was a much older man and did not carry a handgun, only a carbine. His clothes looked trail-worn, unlike those of his flashy companion. Yet there was little doubt who was in charge. The young gunman relaxed at once and broke out into a forced smile.

'Caught me on the hop there, stranger. Weren't expecting anyone else to be here. Lucky for you my *amigo* called out, otherwise you might have got yourself killed.'

'Perhaps,' smiled Harry.

'Anyway, no harm done,' said the man on horseback. 'Mrs Foster, now I see you got some help, and as you don't want to sell out yet, we will be on our way. But we will be back; until then, good day to you both.'

He turned his horse and rode slowly away. The young rider mounted his horse, a pinto. He glowered angrily at Harry, then rode swiftly after his companion, digging his big Mexican spurs cruelly into the pinto's flanks. The fierce expression on the young gunfighter's face made Mary worry for Harry's safety.

'I think you've made a bad enemy there,' she said.

'The other one is more dangerous,' Harry replied as they walked back into the house. 'That kid is all for show.'

Although he could still not remember anything more about his past, he had not felt in any way challenged by the young gunman. The newly acquired Navy Colt felt as if it had always belonged to him, but was he any good with it? He needed to find out without alarming Mary.

He might practise as he rode round the homestead repairing fences, if only he had a saddle. He mentioned the problem to Mary during the evening meal. She smiled and offered him a second helping of apple-pie which he was unable to refuse. He could not remember when he had last eaten so well.

'I'm glad to see your appetite has returned,' she said. 'The more you eat, the sooner you will start to regain your strength. Only then can you start thinking about riding round the ranch.'

Mary refused to discuss the matter further. Reluctantly Harry was forced to agree that she was right. As usual, he felt very tired, so he retired early. Next morning he received a surprise as he walked into the kitchen. In spite of her statement the night before, there was a saddle on the table instead of breakfast.

Mary smiled at him and began to cook breakfast. Bacon and eggs, far better fare than he was used to having in the Confederate Army. During his service for them he had often gone without food for days. Half-remembered experiences flashed into his mind, but he could not hold on to them. Somehow he had fought for both sides in the Civil War. Unfortunately, before he could make any sense of his new recollections they were gone, driven out by Mary as she spoke.

'The saddle belonged to my husband,' she said. 'It's only been gathering dust in the barn, so you might as well put it to use while you're here.'

Mary's statement did not ring true. The whole rig was in superb condition. The leather of the saddle was soft and supple, so it must have been oiled and polished frequently and not left to gather dust in the barn, as she had said. What she had to gain from this falsehood mystified Harry and drove the half-remembered recollections of his time in the Confederate Army out of his mind.

After breakfast he saddled up Mary's pony. Used only for pulling the gig, the animal did not take kindly to the procedure. First it kicked out wildly as he fastened the saddle. Then it began to buck viciously as he tried to mount it. Yet its antics caused him few problems. Within a few minutes he had pacified the animal. Had he once been a horse-handler or wrangler? He simply could not remember.

Although not large enough to be called a ranch or plantation, Mary's home was at least four times larger than the normal eighty-acre homestead. It was a beautiful spring morning, the heat of the sun made comfortable by a cooling breeze, so Harry was in no hurry as he rode. Indeed, he frequently dismounted to practise shooting.

At first his aim was poor, his draw slow and awkward. So it seemed his confidence in facing the young gunman had been misplaced. It was not until the afternoon that it began to come back. During his fourth session he began to hit everything dead centre, even when he fired from his hip.

He returned to the house just before

nightfall, tired but well satisfied. Although she must have heard him shooting, to his surprise Mary did not question him about it.

It took him three days to get it all back. By then he had confirmed his original feelings. He was accurate and exceptionally fast. He needed only a little more practice to be more than a match for all but the very best.

The next visitor to the homestead was old Doc Evans. As often as he could he visited Mary to keep an eye on her as he had promised Mary's father before he died. He had heard the news that Mary had hired a new hand, and came to check that everything was all right. Grey-haired, bespectacled and approaching sixty, the doctor was still a sprightly man.

A much-respected and well-loved doctor, he was a noted rifleman. A Texan, he had served with considerable distinction in the Texas War of Independence (from Mexico). A committed abolitionist during the Civil War, he fought for the Union against the South, which was why he had never returned to Texas.

He had risen to the rank of Chief Field Surgeon under Mary's father, who had been a colonel. Since her father's death he had regarded Mary as his own daughter, and there was a deep bond of affection between them. It seemed only natural she should confide in him. As a result he gave Harry a thorough check-up. While he did so, Mary busied herself in the kitchen preparing an early dinner.

'Well, young man, in spite of the time you spent as the Barfly, there seems nothing physically wrong with you.'

'What about my loss of memory?' asked Harry.

'Not so unusual,' replied the doctor. 'I came across it several times during the Civil War. It can be caused by something as simple as a blow to the head, but in most of the cases I dealt with it appeared to have been caused by the blast from an explosion.'

'Did the memory return?' asked Harry.

'Yes, in all but one case. But it was not due to any treatment I gave. Each time the memory seemed to come back of its own accord, in its own good time. Most returned within a few days, others took months. As I say, only one failed to return.'

'Dinner's ready,' called Mary from the kitchen.

Over dinner they continued to discuss Harry's loss of memory. Harry recounted the two brief flashes of his past and how they seemed to contradict each other. Mary, on the other hand, seemed more concerned about the time Harry spent as the Barfly.

'I think it may be a sign that your memory is on the mend, but don't try yet to make sense of the things you remember,' said the doctor, adopting his best bedside manner. 'Think of your recollections as disconnected pages from a book. It may only make sense after they all return, when you've read the book, as it were. That could be tomorrow, a month, a year, or even longer.'

'Any idea what caused Harry to become the Barfly?' asked Mary.

'None. It's something I've never encountered before, so I can't tell you if it's likely to happen again. Although there's no medical reason to suppose it will,' Doc Evans added hastily.

No matter how they tried, Doc Evans would not discuss the matter further, except to say that Harry no longer looked like the Barfly, and that his new appearance might help to prevent him reverting to his former character.

After the doctor had gone, Mary touched up the roots of Harry's hair which were beginning to show their natural colour. Far from being embarrassed by having his hair coloured, Harry enjoyed the treatment. Perhaps the nearness of Mary had something to do with it.

Neglect and the ravages of the previous winter meant there was plenty of work to do. Harry spent most of his time repairing the perimeter fences, replacing posts and restringing the wire. He was glad to see that Mary did not use barbed wire. He had the cowboy's instinctive hatred of barbed wire, although he had no recollection of working on a big ranch.

Mary kept herself busy around the house, milking the cows and collecting the eggs. However, she needed to take the proceeds into Redrock. So most days Harry had to return to the house by midday, unsaddle the pony, then hitch it up to the gig so Mary could drive to town. Although he found plenty of odd jobs to do around the house and barn, the important work was out on the range. There was only one thing for it; they had to buy another horse, not least because they were seriously overworking Mary's pony.

Mary had only sixty dollars saved but insisted on giving it to Harry to buy another horse. As he had no money of his own, he accepted the offer, but only on the condition that he would not receive any pay until he had worked off the amount. At least the deal gave credence to the story they had concocted for his sudden appearance at the homestead.

Next morning, instead of checking out the rest of the fences, he helped Mary. Much to his surprise he found he knew how to milk cows and quickly filled two churns while Mary collected the eggs.

As soon as they arrived at Redrock, Mary drove to the store. While she delivered the milk and eggs, Harry made his way to the livery stables. After her last experience with the big blacksmith, Mary had no wish to meet Brad again.

As he walked into the stable, Harry paused to read a poster offering a hundred dollar reward for the capture of the Barfly, dead or alive. The drawing on the poster was even more grotesque than he had actually been. Anyone seeing him now would not connect him with it. His only problem was that, as the Barfly, he had slept in the livery stable and worked in the saloon. As the blacksmith also ran the livery stable, he was one of the two men in Redrock most likely to recognize him.

'Don't suppose you've seen the ugly sod?'

Harry had been so engrossed in the poster he had failed to notice Brad as he came up behind him, the blacksmith's face still bearing the marks of his fight with the Barfly. However, as Harry turned to face the giant, there was no sign of recognition on his battered face.

'Sorry, no,' replied Harry.

'Anyway, stranger, the name's Brad. What can I do for you?'

'I'm looking to buy a horse. Mine broke its leg in a gopher-hole. It never did have a lick of sense but I'm lost without it.'

Brad looked at Harry's Texas-style boots which were clearly made for riding, not walking. He also noted the ease with which the man in front of him carried his revolver. Word of the arrival of a stranger at Mary's homestead had spread throughout Redrock, as had his willingness to face out Bill Gordon. Flashy as Gordon was, his speed with a six-gun had won him grudging respect, in spite of his tender years.

'Reckon you must be the new man at Mary's homestead,' said Brad, remembering his treatment of Mary last time they met.

'That's right, the name is Harry Brown. Now what about a horse?'

'Well. I ain't going to fool you,' said Brad, looking at Harry's six-gun. 'Most of what I got for sale are mustangs. I'll take thirty-five dollars for any of them. Don't get much call for quality horses, but you're welcome to check out what I've got.'

Harry did just that, only to discover the blacksmith did not have a decent horse amongst his remuda. Never had he seen a poorer bunch of horses in his life, and he had bought many in his time. No, he would not have used any of them on the Shawnee trail. Some trail herds stampeded without warning, then a man's life might well depend on a good horse or pony.

He had remembered another fragment from his past. Perhaps he had once been a drover driving cattle up the old Shawnee trail, or maybe he had been a wrangler looking after the remudas of horses used during the trail drive? If so, it must have been before the Civil War, since the state of Missouri had long since closed its borders to the mighty herds of Texas longhorns. His only memories of the Civil War were still as confused as ever. From the little he could remember, it seemed he had fought for both sides, but how could that have been?

He was not allowed to dwell on the problem for long. The sound of a horse neighing reminded him of the job in hand. The sound had not come from the broken-down nags in front of him, and they began to reply to a horse behind him. He turned round and saw the big blacksmith gingerly leading a large palomino stallion into the livery stable. The stallion's sleek body was the colour of champagne, light golden brown. In contrast its mane and tail were snowy white. Clearly of Arabic descent, it was a magnificent beast, yet from the way it pulled against its bit, difficult to control. In spite of his massive size, the big blacksmith seemed to be more than a little afraid of the magnificent palomino. Harry had no such fear and took an instant liking to the spirited animal.

'For sale?' asked Harry.

'A bit too wild for most,' said Brad, as he struggled to control the horse.

'How much?'

'Couldn't take less than a hundred and fifty for him. You see, it's not my horse; I'm selling him for a friend.'

'Sorry,' replied Harry, and shrugged his shoulders.

'Sixty is my top limit, it's my boss,

Mrs Foster's money, not mine.'

At the mention of Mary's name, a crafty look came over the blacksmith's face. Roughly, he quieted the palomino, then turned to face Harry.

'Tell you what, stranger. I could make you a sort of deal. I'll take fifty bucks down, no — make it sixty — and I'll throw in a saddle. If you can ride her down Main Street in, well, let's say in ten days, she's yours and I'll have to make up the difference to my friend. If not, you bring her back and take a mustang, then work in my stable for a week.'

Something in the blacksmith's attitude warned Harry against taking the bet. Yet the palomino was a fine horse, a bargain at even two hundred dollars. At worst he would pay over the odds for a mustang and have to muck out the stable for a week. Even a broken-down nag would be better than none, and he could work off the money he wasted. The idea of having to stay longer at the homestead was not so unappealing. In fact, the prospect made up his mind.

'You got yourself a deal,' he said, and shook hands on it.

Education was still in its infancy in the West. Most could neither read nor write. A man was judged by the way he kept his word, and a handshake sealed a deal better than a written contract. Harry paid over the money and Brad fetched a saddle. He seemed to take a long time, but Harry did not mind, it gave him the chance to get to know the palomino.

'Of course, you know your own business best,' said the giant blacksmith, 'but give the horse a chance to get to know you before you try to ride him. I want you to have a chance to win the bet.'

'What's his name?' asked Harry.

'Goldwind.'

Harry took the blacksmith's advice, slung the saddle over his left shoulder and led the palomino to the store. Mary was waiting in the gig for him. For Harry's sake she appeared delighted with the bet, but she knew to her cost that Brad was not to be trusted.

However, she concealed her doubts and decided to try to persuade Harry not to ride the palomino until she had spoken to the doctor. She made an excuse to stop at his house, leaving Harry to look after the gig and Goldwind. Unfortunately, the doctor was out, so she left a message explaining what had happened.

Mary drove slowly on the way back, so by the time they reached the homestead, it was too late for Harry to try to ride Goldwind.

Next day she insisted that he should catch up on the work on the fences not done the previous day. It rained hard during the next morning, making work impossible. When the rain finally stopped, Mary sent Harry into town to deliver the milk and eggs. Finally she ran out of excuses to prevent Harry from riding Goldwind and still she had not heard from Dr Evans.

Goldwind had been a model of good

behaviour until Harry put the blacksmith's saddle on the palomino. He had thought that it would be better to use a saddle familiar to the horse, rather than the one Mary had given him. He could not have been more wrong.

He had barely tightened up the girth when Goldwind began to play up. His first attempt to ride Goldwind lasted barely five seconds. The palomino bucked, rolled, then jack-knifed. Harry found himself flying through the air until he hit the ground with a thud.

It was his pride rather than his body that was injured, so he picked himself up and tried again. A few seconds later, he was back on the ground, this time with all the wind knocked out of him. He did no better the third and fourth time. He was about to try yet again when Dr Evans arrived in his buggy.

He had been delivering a baby at one of the big ranches situated on the other side of Redrock when Mary called at his town surgery. It had been a difficult birth and there had been complications which had prevented him coming to the homestead until now.

Over a cup of coffee, he explained the trick the blacksmith had played on Harry. It was one he had done many times before. No one had ever managed to stay on Goldwind for more than a few seconds. Several unsuspecting buyers had finished up paying a ridiculously high price for one of Brad's broken down old nags.

That night Harry could not sleep. There had to be a way to ride Goldwind, for he was sure the palomino was not a rogue horse. A similar situation had happened in his past, but the details remained out of reach. Finally, he drifted off into a fitful sleep. When he awoke at dawn, he remembered.

He went to the barn and fed Goldwind. The palomino was friendly and seemed pleased to see him. While the horse was eating, Harry carefully inspected him. After a few minutes he found what he had been looking for, and an expression of pure disgust crossed his face.

Swiftly, he went outside and hunted around until he found some wild leaves, which he ground to a pulp. Very gently he applied the concoction to Goldwind's back and repeated the process every four hours. He continued the process for the next two days until he was sure Goldwind had fully recovered. Finally he checked the saddle Brad had given him. It did not take long to confirm that his suspicions were correct.

The day appointed for Harry to ride Goldwind down Main Street duly arrived. It was Saturday. Redrock was full of folks waiting to see Brad's latest victim. Harry did not keep them waiting long, arriving well before noon; however, not on Goldwind, but with Mary in the gig. The palomino trotted behind, but without a saddle. The many onlookers, crowded along the sidewalks of Main Street, voiced their disappointment, as it looked as if the stranger was not going to try to win the bet.

Hearing the commotion outside his livery stable, Brad came out to investigate. His eyes lit up when he saw the unsaddled Goldwind. Like the rest of the onlookers he also thought Harry had given up on the bet. However, he was wrong.

Harry called to Goldwind and jumped from the gig on to the back of the palomino. Much to the surprise of the crowd, the big stallion trotted obediently up Main Street and back again. The onlookers broke out into a chorus of cheers; Brad was not a popular person. But the huge blacksmith was not ready to concede defeat.

'Hold on!' he cried out over the tumult, 'I didn't say nothing about riding bareback like a damned Injun! The bet was to ride it, civilized and proper-like, with a saddle.'

The crowd's mood swung round rapidly to favour the blacksmith. Calmly Harry dismounted and took the saddle which Mary had given him from the back of the gig and put it on Goldwind. The big palomino accepted the saddle without any fuss and the ride was repeated without incident.

Amid the cheers of the crowd, Harry dismounted and retrieved Brad's saddle which was also in the back of the gig. Immediately, Goldwind reared, then started to paw the ground with his front legs. For no apparent reason the big palomino suddenly became very aggressive.

Doc Evans had been watching the events. Fascinated, like most of Redrock's citizens, he had no idea what Harry was going to do next. Slowly, Harry carried the blacksmith's saddle over to him.

'Care to examine the saddle?' he asked the doctor.

Puzzled by Harry's action and Goldwind's sudden change of attitude, the crowd grew silent. The bespectacled doctor examined the saddle as carefully as if it was one of his patients.

Suddenly, his hand appeared from

under the saddle, grasping a tiny spur. It was perfect in every detail, yet so small, few in the crowd could see it. However, those nearest the doctor could see his palm bleeding — a testament to the sharpness of the tiny spur's rowels.

An angry growl spread through the crowd as they realized how the blacksmith duped his victims. The growl turned to a roar of approval as Harry dropped the saddle and unstrapped his gun belt.

'Now I've another bet for you,' Harry said, staring coldly at Brad. 'If you can whip me, you get your horse back and keep the money. Should I win, your saddle goes on your back and someone gets to ride you, up and down Main Street.'

The mood of the crowd gave Brad little option. To save face and stay in business, he had to accept Harry's challenge. Not that he was concerned about the outcome. True, somehow the Barfly had beaten him, but nobody else had come close.

Brimming with confidence, Brad rushed Harry. After that, everything happened with bewildering speed. In less than five minutes the fight was over. The big blacksmith lay on the ground, bruised, bloodied and utterly defeated. Harry stood over him, unmarked and scarcely out of breath. He had defeated Brad when he had been the drunken Barfly; now stronger and fitter, he was far too quick for the lumbering blacksmith.

At first the crowd fell silent, overawed by the ease of Harry's victory, but their mood changed rapidly. They began to roar their approval as one of the blacksmith's former victims grabbed the saddle and strapped it on the luckless smith's back.

The six-guns pointed at his head prevented the battered blacksmith from protesting, as his former victim jumped on to the saddle. The blacksmith was then forced to crawl to the end of Main Street and back with the saddle, and rider, on his back.

When the ordeal was over, the saddle was removed. The back of Brad's shirt was soaked in blood, indicating there had been more of the tiny but vicious spurs left in the saddle.

After his ordeal, Brad was taken to Doc Evans's surgery. The crowd treated him roughly, showing little sympathy. However, the doctor treated his cuts with care, but used medicine distilled from wild plants to prevent infection. The old Indian remedy usually worked but stung wickedly. Brad's roars of pain were audible all over Redrock, much to the amusement of its townsfolk.

Harry, now the undisputed owner of Goldwind, rode out of Redrock on the superb stallion, his popularity well established. Mary followed in the gig, but before they reached the homestead, they saw a column of dense black smoke rising into the air.

Harry raced Goldwind back to the homestead, leaving the gig far behind. In their absence, someone had set the barn alight. As he reached it he could see the fire was out of control. There was little he could do except watch the fire destroy what was left of the barn. By the time Mary arrived in the gig, the building was a smouldering ruin.

3

The lone rider saw the billowing smoke rising into the clear blue sky. Although he was too far away to see the barn, he guessed the smoke came from a burning building. A guess born from bitter experience. During the Civil War he had seen many homesteads and plantations burnt to the ground. Not that he was an innocent in such matters, for he had put the torch to many a fine home, his own plantation included. Yet it had all been for nothing, the Union Army had never come to grips with their adversaries, the 43rd Irregulars, or Mosby's Confederacy as they were better known. Now their leader, General Mosby, was a high ranking diplomat for the US Government, while he was an outcast.

That had been the price he, a Southerner, had paid for fighting for the Union. A price he continued to pay, for when the madness, which had set brother against brother, had finally ended, for him there had been only bitter recriminations. Although he had been acting under orders, his family had never forgiven him.

So he left the remains of his plantation in the care of a cousin and moved West, earning a living using skills honed to perfection during the Civil War. He could follow a trail better than most Indians and use the Remington .44 slung low in his holster better than anybody he had met so far.

The letter in his pocket indicated there was someone in Redrock prepared to pay well for those skills. Luke Donovan was a bounty hunter, even if he did not look like most people's idea of one.

If he had abandoned the South, neither the Civil War nor his current disreputable profession had altered his standards. Even though he fought for the abolition of slavery, Luke Donovan still considered himself to be a gentleman and dressed like one. He rode swiftly towards the rising smoke to see if he could offer any assistance; a Southern gentleman could do no less.

As he drew nearer to the black column of smoke, his trained eyes espied two riders on a distant ridge. From their vantage-point they must have been able to see the source of the smoke, yet they did not move. Luke formed the impression they were looking at the result of their handiwork, although he had nothing but a gut feeling to go on. However, that gut feeling was reinforced when the two riders turned away from the fire and cantered out of sight down the other side of the ridge.

His past experiences of fires had taught him to expect the worst, but as he drew nearer the homestead, he could see it was only the barn which had been burning. He could also see the figures of a man and woman standing by the smouldering remains.

He slowed Josh, his big black stallion, to a walking pace, surmising the owners of the homestead were apt to be suspicious of strangers. Rushing in now might invite a bullet by mistake.

'Hello, the house,' he shouted, 'need any help?'

'Not much anybody can do,' replied Harry.

Harry was right. The fire had all but burnt itself out. Luke approached slowly, then dismounted. Keeping all his movements slow, the bounty-hunter deliberately held his gun hand well away from his six-gun, so as not to give cause for alarm.

Josh snorted angrily. He had seen Goldwind, a stallion to rival him. However, the big palomino simply ignored the new arrival, as there were no mares around to fight over.

'They call me Luke Donovan. Looks like you good folk have a heap of trouble. Any idea who started the fire?'

'What makes you think it didn't start naturally?' asked Mary.

'The two riders on yonder ridge. They were just watching, then instead of riding to help you, they rode away.'

'There's nothing to be gained standing around,' said Mary. 'Mr Donovan, if you will give Harry a hand to dampen down the fire, I'll cook us all dinner.'

Both Harry and Luke were experienced enough not to ask each other questions. As a result they worked in silence until Mary called to tell them dinner was ready. Even so, both men tended to the needs of their horses before entering the house. Luke also insisted on washing thoroughly before he ate.

After dinner, they made small talk. Luke suggested to Harry he might repair the water-pump in the yard, so it could be used in the event of further outbreaks of fire. He noticed Harry became evasive about anything in his past, but Luke's code of honour dictated he kept off any topic likely to embarrass his host. He was surprised to discover Harry was only the hired hand,

and not Mary's husband. Her attitude towards Harry had initially led him to believe otherwise.

As evening drew near, Luke made to leave. He thought it likely Harry was a wanted man, perhaps with a bounty on his head. Since collecting bounties was his business, he did not want to become too friendly in case Harry turned out to be the man he had been hired to catch.

'I'm sorry that I can't offer to put you up,' apologized Mary.

'Think nothing of it,' Luke replied. 'I have business in Redrock which needs attending to. Perhaps I'll see you there?'

As Harry watched Luke ride off, he thought there was much more to Luke than met the eye. As Luke turned and waved goodbye, he thought the same of Harry.

According to the letter, Luke's benefactor had already reserved a room for him in Redrock's only hotel, so there was little need to hurry. It was more important to get the lie of the land and discover if there were any hidden valleys or water-holes near the trail where a wanted man might hide out. Although he did not find any, it was time well spent. His livelihood depended upon his ability to track down wanted men before any of his rivals.

So far Luke had earned about four thousand dollars in bounty money, but his expenses had been high. Nevertheless, he had banked half of it. A tidy sum, but not nearly enough to let him rebuild his plantation and resume his former lifestyle. So if there was a reward for Harry, he would collect it. It mattered little that he liked the man. Personal feelings were something a bounty-hunter could ill afford.

It was late evening when he finally arrived in Redrock. Later still by the time he had dealt with Josh. Because the blacksmith was unfit to work, Luke had to unsaddle the big stallion, rub him down and finally feed him.

The saloon was still buzzing about Brad's latest fight, so Luke found it easy to find out about Harry's mysterious arrival at Mary's homestead. Satisfied he had learned all he could for the night, Luke finally checked into the hotel.

In common with most hotels in the West, Redrock's only hotel insisted all cowboys, or anybody else covered in trail grime, must bathe before they were allowed to go to their room. However, it was late, so there was no hot water. It would have taken at least an hour to build up the fire and heat up enough water to fill the bath. All extra work for the desk clerk.

Luke waved the clerk's half-hearted objections aside. It had been a long day and he was tired. Prudently, the night porter concluded that Luke was not a man to rile by insisting on a rule, so went back to reading his paper.

Luke ordered a bath next morning, after which he put on his other set of clothes. Following a remarkably good breakfast, he left the hotel and went searching for the barber's shop. In a small town like Redrock it was not hard to find. Going regularly to the barber for an early-morning shave was the best way of getting information. Whatever the town, its barber was usually only too willing to discuss everyone else's business.

Luke made a point of using his first visit to feed the barber information he wanted generally known about himself. He used roughly the same cover-story for each new town he visited.

People disliked bounty-hunters in their town, not least because they brought the violence of their profession with them. Many rewards were offered on a dead-or-alive basis, with the emphasis on dead. Killing the wanted man saved the State the expense of a trial. It also saved the bounty-hunter the trouble of returning the outlaw to the place where he committed the crime, often a dangerous and time-consuming business.

During his shave, Luke casually told the barber he was looking for property on behalf of his business partner. This led to the barber suggesting the livery stable and smithy might be up for sale. This was not because Brad had been so soundly thrashed by Harry, nor even because he had been exposed as a cheat, but who would trust the man with their horses, after he had caused Goldwind so much unnecessary suffering in order to win bets?

The barber confirmed what Luke had already found out about Harry, then went on to talk about the mysterious disappearance of the man the townsfolk had called the Barfly.

Were these events in any way connected with Luke's business in Redrock? Perhaps, for the letter tied in nicely with another wanted man he had been after. The last report he received about his quarry indicated the man had been seen heading in the direction of Redrock. After that the man had disappeared, just about the same time as Harry had mysteriously arrived in Redrock.

If Harry was indeed the same man, he might well prove to be dangerous, for the man Luke wanted had ridden with Quantrill's Raiders during the Civil War. After the South had surrendered, President Lincoln decreed there must be no retaliation against anyone who had fought for the Confederacy, with the exception of those who had served under Quantrill.

Although Quantrill had been killed before the end of the War, he and his men were accused of waging their own private war. It was said they committed atrocities against civilians from both the Union and the South. Luke did not know the details, nor did he care. All that mattered to him was the $1,000 bounty offered for the man's capture, dead or alive.

Well content with the morning's work, he left the barber and headed down Main Street to the sheriff's office. It was politic to make the town sheriff aware of his arrival, so Luke made a habit of getting to know the law in each town he visited.

The pay of most small-town sheriff's was poor, usually between forty and fifty dollars a month, plus keep. To make matters worse, many lawmen were expected to provide their own ammunition. So it was not surprising some lawmen found ways to increase their income.

Some made extra money by offering a protection service to one or more of the saloons in their town. Others failed to apprehend wanted men who commanded a good reward for their capture. Instead, they sent for a bounty-hunter to do the job. When the reward money was issued, the lawman took his cut. As long as the bounty-hunter signed a statement agreeing he had received all the reward money, there was little the authorities could do.

Provided the lawman involved was not too greedy, Luke was happy to enter into such arrangements, as they saved him weeks spent tracking down fugitives. Since the lawman was getting a cut of the bounty, he was normally only too happy to quickly verify the identification of the wanted man, necessary before the reward money could be paid.

Luke had no idea how widespread this practice was, but he had similar arrangements with five different lawmen. However, Ben Webster, Redrock's sheriff, was not one of them. This time the information had come from the town's mayor, Jeremiah Grande.

He was in no hurry to meet the mayor. It was more important to meet the town's lawmen and gauge their ability. He walked to the sheriff's office and introduced himself.

It did not take him long to decide it was Deputy Zack Blake, not Ben Webster, who made all the important decisions. It seemed all the sheriff wanted was a quiet life and to pick up his pay-check at the end of each month. His brash young deputy was a different proposition. Blake made it clear he welcomed the chance to add to the four notches already on his gun-butt, without actually threatening Luke directly.

However, both lawmen were adamant there were no wanted men in Redrock, nor were they aware of any properties for sale. Blake also implied that while Luke was welcome to stay for a few days, he would be well advised not to outstay his welcome.

Luke had heard it all before, many times, so he merely smiled and left. Something about the set-up bothered him. It was not just that Zack Blake was actually in charge, but why should such an obviously ambitious young man choose to be a deputy in a sleepy town like Redrock? Besides, no one living solely on a deputy's pay could afford such expensive clothes and a pearl-handled six-gun.

Luke was so preoccupied with his thoughts, he did not look where he was going and bumped into a young woman, almost knocking her down. Without thinking, he grabbed her to stop her falling. Yet it was not their collision that took his breath away, but her sparkling blue eyes and her long hair, the colour of sun-ripened corn.

'I'm so sorry,' he gasped. 'Are you all right?'

'I'm fine, so you can let go of me now, if you don't mind.'

In his confusion, he had not realized he was still gripping her tightly around her waist. He let go so quickly, she was taken by surprise and started to fall again. He grabbed her for the second time.

'Now let's try that again,' she said coldly. 'Only this time, let go a little more slowly and I'll try not to fall. Otherwise we'll be here all day.

Red-faced, Luke did as he was told. She brushed herself down, then walked quickly away before he could think of anything to say. He watched her walk down Main Street. Dressed in a dark brown, ankle-length dress, matching boots and gloves, she looked a picture of elegance. Luke shook himself angrily and turned away. From her demeanour and the way she dressed, it was clear that she was far removed from the saloon girls with whom he normally associated.

Still angry with himself, he walked briskly towards the hotel and entered without looking behind him. Had he done so, he could not have failed to see the young woman stop, slowly turn and watch him walk into the hotel. Far from looking angry, a smile spread slowly across her face.

Luke spent the rest of the day familiarizing himself with Redrock and the surrounding countryside. He would have liked to talk to the blacksmith, usually another reliable source of information. However, Brad had not put in an appearance since he lost the fight and bet. Yet if Brad's sudden disappearance bothered the sheriff, he did nothing about it. Doing nothing seemed to be Ben Webster's response to most things.

Next day, a young lad called John

temporarily took over the running of the stables. Although the boy was too inexperienced to operate the forge, he appeared to be a good horse-handler and the arrangement seemed to please Luke's horse Josh. The black stallion loved being groomed, and the boy was doing a thorough job on him when Luke called in to see how Josh was being treated.

Well satisfied with the attention Josh was receiving, Luke made his way to the barber for his morning shave. However, he learned nothing new, the barber seemed unusually reticent. Had Zack Blake visited the barber and discouraged him from talking to Luke?

After his shave, Luke visited the town hall to make an appointment to see the mayor. He did not need one, as Jeremiah Grande agreed to see him immediately. Luke was ushered into a small, functional office. From his greeting, it seemed the mayor had been expecting him, although his welcome was guarded and he kept up Luke's pretence of looking for property.

'Good morning, Mr Donovan. Word has it that you are seeking a place round here. We certainly need more people to settle here, so is there anything I can do to help?'

Jeremiah Grande was a stout, stocky man, about forty years old. His curly hair was jet black, but there was more than a hint of grey in his long sideburns. He was dressed smartly in a long black jacket, grey trousers, black shoes. Yet he wore a light-blue shirt and a bright-blue necktie. If his clothes were formal, they were certainly not dull. There was something in his frank, open eyes and confident manner that Luke took to at once. He was about to ask the mayor about the letter when they were interrupted.

The door swung open and a man walked in. The mayor jumped to his feet. The man was as unlike Jeremiah Grande as it was possible to be. He was tall and, although he had a marked stoop, he still towered over the mayor.

He wore a gaudy uniform. Blue tunic with yellow epaulettes and insignia that denoted he had once been a colonel. The colours of his Cavalry trousers were yellow with a blue strip, the reverse of those now worn by the recently reinstated US Cavalry.

The colonel made no apology for interrupting them. Luke doubted whether the man had ever apologized in his entire life. His attitude was extremely arrogant and he completely ignored Luke, as he addressed the mayor.

'When you have a minute, Jeremiah, I want to see you.'

The words were spoken in a precise manner, clipped tight as was the fashion in New England. Yet the man's attire suggested he had a very different origin. In spite of his words, it was clear from his arrogant manner he expected the mayor to get rid of Luke immediately and attend to him.

'As soon as I have finished business with Mr Donovan,' replied the mayor.

'Perhaps you would like to be introduced to him? He's looking round the district for property.'

The colonel looked at Luke as if he were something rather disgusting the cat had just dragged in. His attitude suggested Luke was the last person he would want as a neighbour.

'Some other time, perhaps. For the moment, Jeremiah, we have important business to discuss.'

The colonel swept out of the room without so much as a glance at Luke. The mayor shrugged his shoulders, as if to acknowledge defeat, then ushered Luke to the door.

'Please accept my apologies, Mr Donovan, but you see how it is,' he said sadly. Then his face brightened as an idea struck him.

'Perhaps you would care to have dinner at my home tonight? Afterwards we can discuss our real business over a glass of brandy or whiskey. If you don't know the way, anyone will direct you.'

As there was little else to do, Luke

went to the saloon for a beer. The saloon was virtually empty, so there was little chance of picking up any new information. After a second beer he returned to the hotel, ordered a light meal, then a bath.

Two baths in the same week were a rare luxury for a man who spent most of his time on the trail. Afterwards, he relaxed in his room. The war years had taught him to rest whenever he could, regardless of the time of day.

A little over an hour later, he saddled Josh and rode out of town, following the directions given to him by John the stable lad. Jeremiah Grande's spread seemed smaller in area than Mary's extended homestead, but the house was much larger. Made of wood and painted white, the house reminded Luke of the plantation houses back home, except he no longer had a home, he reminded himself bitterly.

He approached the house slowly, Josh barely cantering as he rode up the long gravel drive. By the side of the house, and set a little way behind it, was a large stable, out of which emerged a youth. He introduced himself as the brother of John, the stable boy in Redrock, then led the big black stallion away.

As Luke entered the large oak-panelled hall, he was met by Jeremiah Grande. Not only had he arrived before Luke, but he had changed into clothes more suited to a cowboy than a mayor. Although he was in the house, he wore a large, ten-gallon hat, so Luke kept on his more modest Stetson. The mayor's town garments had been replaced by Levis and a bright-red shirt.

'Come in, my boy. Sit yourself down while I pour you a drink. At least we won't be interrupted in here.'

The mayor ushered Luke into what appeared to be a library. Certainly he had never seen so many books in one room.

'I must apologize for the interruption this morning,' continued the mayor, 'but Colonel Masters considers himself to be a busy man and expects everyone to dance to his tune. Unfortunately, as he owns most of the county and half of the town, the rest of us have little choice.'

'I don't think I understand,' said Luke, as he sipped the excellent brandy he had been offered.

'The colonel owns the hotel, the newspaper, the main saloon and the largest spread around Redrock,' replied the mayor. 'But let's change the subject and we'll talk about something more interesting.'

'Well, I'd like to discuss the letter you sent me,' said Luke.

'That can wait until after dinner,' said Mrs Grande as she entered the library. 'Jeremiah, you have not shown our guest to his room. Shame on you, husband. Mr Donovan will be wanting to wash before he eats and dinner will be ready in a few minutes.'

A twinkle in her eyes and the lilt in her voice softened her words. Although well past the first flush of youth, Mrs Grande was still an attractive woman. The few wrinkles around her blue eyes and the odd wisp of white amongst her deep blonde hair merely added distinction to her natural beauty. She reminded Luke of someone he had met before, but who that was, he could not say.

'I had not thought to stay the night, although I thank you for your kind offer,' said Luke, slipping back into his Southern manner of speech.

'Nonsense' retorted Mrs Grande. 'We have too few chances to entertain these days. Besides, Mr Grande will want a chance to show you his horses tomorrow, won't you, dear?'

'Yes, my love,' replied the mayor, dutifully.

Twenty minutes later, Luke found himself in the dining room. From the kitchen came the delightful smell of roast pork. A window looked out on to the small ranch, but it had become too dark for Luke to see much outside, so he turned his attention to the dining room.

Large oil-paintings, depicting herds of buffalo, deer and game, hung on each wall. In the centre of the room stood a magnificent, eight-seater, oak table. At its head sat Jeremiah Grande, still wearing his ten-gallon hat. At the opposite end sat his wife, who had changed into a dark red, formal evening-gown. She looked charming, Luke thought; the mayor was a fortunate man.

As Luke sat down, he noticed that another place had been set opposite him. The cutlery was solid silver, and the matching dinner service was English, not dissimilar to the Crown Derby set he had once possessed. The entire room had an extremely affluent air about it, again reminding Luke of his old home, or how it had once been.

His reflections were interrupted as the kitchen door opened. Carrying a side of pork on a silver platter came the cook, a dark-haired woman of French origin. Luke caught his breath, for behind her, carrying a tray of potatoes and carrots, came the vision of loveliness he had almost knocked over earlier that day. She put the tray down on the table and sat down in the place set directly opposite him.

'Let me introduce my daughter, Elizabeth,' said Mrs Grande.

'We've already met,' she replied, staring hard at Luke, yet there was almost a chuckle in her voice as she continued. 'We sort of bumped into each other in town today.'

Her cornflower-blue eyes seemed to bore right through him. She wore a long black dress that not only empha-sized the blondness of her hair, but clung to her figure so tightly he wondered how she could breathe.

Since he had left the South and became a successful bounty-hunter, Luke usually had enough money to secure the favours of any woman who could be bought. Although there was one 'soiled dove' he returned to

80

whenever he could, there had never been any deep commitment between them. Until now he had never felt any desire to settle down. Yet as he looked at Elizabeth, he began to wish he was not a bounty-hunter. Perhaps his old way of life would never return, and now was the time to start thinking about a new future?

Back in the security of his room that night, he could recall little of the meal or the conversation. Yet he could remember the exact moment he had finally agreed to stay, not merely for the night, but for the next few days. It had been when Elizabeth had asked him. She had transfixed him with her cornflower-blue eyes and made it seem as if it was important to her that he stayed.

Now, alone in the guest-bedroom, he was almost sure he had imagined it. Time to get a grip on his feelings, for they were a luxury he could not afford. Once Elizabeth found out he was a bounty-hunter she was unlikely to want anything to do with him. But he could dream, couldn't he? Everyone should be allowed one dream, he said to himself as he fell asleep.

Yet it was no dream next morning, when neither Elizabeth nor her father, offered to show him round the stables and the rest of the farm. Apparently her father had received a message that he was urgently needed at the bank.

Luke thought it odd he had not heard anyone ride up to the ranch to deliver the message, but the chance to be with Elizabeth caused him to dismiss it from his mind. Instead, he silently thanked Colonel Masters, whom he assumed to be the cause of the mayor's early departure.

Luke's gratitude increased when another messenger arrived with the rest of his things from the hotel and a message from the mayor. It seemed he would be detained in Redrock over-night and probably most of the next day. It seemed that another homestead had been raided. Unfortunately, it appeared this raid had merely been a ruse. While Sheriff Webster and Deputy Blake had ridden out to investigate the incident, Redrock's only bank had been robbed, and a cashier and two customers had been wounded.

The reason for the raid was a mystery. According to the mayor, the small bank carried little cash. Twice weekly, the stagecoach brought a strong-box containing sufficient funds for trading. In this way it had been hoped to avoid any raids on the town bank. Yet the outlaw gang had ignored the relatively lightly defended stage-coach and raided the bank. All for a few hundred dollars which, when split between the gang, would scarcely be worth the risk.

4

They hit Mary's homestead an hour after noon. Many riders raced towards the house, guns drawn. As they drew nearer they opened fire, their bullets thudding into the house wall, smashing the main window. Harry, busy mending fences in the bottom pasture, heard the shots, sprinted to Goldwind and raced back to the house as quickly as the palomino could carry him.

As luck would have it, he had only just started to work on the fences furthest from the house. Ever since the fire, he had been working to set up a system to prevent anyone burning down the house. He had finished it that morning; now it looked as if his work was to be put to the test as the roof of the outhouse attached to the main house was ablaze. At least one of the raiders had succeeded in throwing a lighted torch on to it.

His first thought was of Mary, but the raiders opened fire preventing him from getting any nearer. Their bullets flew harmlessly wide, the range was too great for accurate shooting.

Harry returned the raiders' fire but the bullets from his Navy Colt fell well short, so he stopped firing and reloaded. Whilst the .38 calibre Colt was a more handy weapon at close range, the .44 Army Colt packed a bigger punch and a longer range.

Harry was outranged and outnumbered. He looked around, desperately seeking cover, then drove Goldwind towards the burnt-out remains of the barn. Bullets flew all around him but his move caught the raiders by surprise and he reached the cover of the ruined barn without being hit. His memory had still not returned, so he had no idea how good he was with a six-gun when under fire. Yet as the raiders' bullets thudded into the charred remains of the barn, he was not afraid. He felt he had been under fire before, even if he could not remember where or when.

He returned their fire but his first two shots were off to the left. His third struck home, and one of the raiders slumped over his saddle. As the other five raiders charged towards him, Harry winged another one, then his last bullet hit a raider full in the chest, knocking him off his horse.

Harry struggled frantically to reload, but the outlaws were on him before he could reopen fire. To his surprise they thundered past, it seemed they had done enough. He completed reloading, then emptied his gun at the fleeing raiders, but the galloping horses sent ash from the burnt-out barn swirling into the air, so he was unable to tell if he had hit any of them.

Taking advantage of the blinding dust, Harry raced out of the barn and into the house. The heat from the blazing outhouse roof was almost unbearable. He found Mary semi-conscious under the dining table. She appeared to be uninjured so he guessed she had been overcome by the choking smoke. Half-dragging, half-carrying, he hauled her outside.

The raiders did not return, apparently content their work was done. Harry left Mary lying on the ground and raced over to the pump. Still half-blinded by the ash dust, he struggled to fasten the hose to it, then began to pump. But he could not pump and aim the hose at the burning roof at the same time. Barely conscious, Mary was unable to help.

To have any chance of saving the house, he had to be cruel. Praying she would forgive him, he turned the hose towards her and started to pump. At first he missed, but after several attempts, he succeeded in directing the cold water over her. She struggled to her feet, only to be hit full in the face by a jet of cold water. She staggered, then fell, but the cold water revived her.

Harry stopped pumping. Coughing and spluttering, Mary scrambled to her feet. She saw Harry's problem and grabbed the hose. As he began pumping again, she aimed the nozzle at the burning roof.

The column of water shot towards the flames. The air, only just beginning to clear from the ashes kicked up by the raiders' horses, filled with smoke and steam. The noise was frightening. Mary thought Hell could be no worse, yet it took them only a few minutes to put out the fire.

Harry was relieved he had acted on Luke's advice and repaired the pump. So virtually all the fire-damage had been confined to the outhouse at the back of the kitchen. Unfortunately, the kitchen floor was covered in water, and the whole house was full of smoke.

Not that they cared. Mary salvaged some food from the kitchen while Harry saddled her pony and Goldwind. They rode across the pastures, through the unfinished fence and on to a place Mary called Two Bit Woods. Really it was no more than a grove of trees. A brook ran through the middle of the grove. During the summer the brook all but dried up, but now in late spring it was in full flood.

Filthy and hungry, they camped for the night. Harry was almost certain the raiders were not about to return, so he lit a fire. Mary cooked a makeshift meal which they ate in silence. They were exhausted, too tired and bewildered to talk.

That night Harry made a point of bedding down on the opposite side of the fire to Mary. He watched her settle down for the night. Sleeping rough had been part of his life during and since the Civil War, yet it was Mary who seemed more at ease, and she immediately fell asleep.

He intended to stand guard over her. Unfortunately, he was still far from his old self, whatever that was, and exhaustion soon overtook him. In spite of his good intentions, he fell into a deep dreamless sleep.

* ★ ★

When he awoke, Mary lay snuggled up in his arms, although he had not moved from his side of the fire. She was also awake, but if she was embarrassed by the intimacy of their position, she gave no sign. Instead, she snuggled even closer, as the sun began to rise.

Mary lay in Harry's arms, feelings of conflicting emotions running through her. It was too soon. In his confused state she knew Harry was not ready to make any kind of commitment. If she allowed anything to happen now, he might just believe she acted like this all the time, and think her little better than a saloon whore. She did not move away, waiting, hoping he would make the first move. When he did not, she snuggled into him even closer.

Surely now he would at least kiss her, she thought? But still he made no move towards her. As the sun began to rise, she realized he was not going to take advantage of the situation. She did not know whether she was relieved or disappointed. Was his lack of action due to respect, or was he simply not interested in her as a woman? Reluctantly, she extricated herself from his arms and stood up. There would be a lot of clearing up to do back at the homestead.

Outside the house, apart from a few blood-splashes on the ground, and the burnt-out roof of the outhouse, there was little to indicate what had happened. Inside it was a different story. In their endeavours to prevent the fire spreading from the outhouse to the main building, they had pumped gallons on to the outhouse roof. As a result, the interiors of both buildings were flooded. Water was everywhere, and the air was still thick with smoke.

Mary set about cleaning while Harry rode into town to report the raid to Sheriff Webster. While he was in Redrock, he went to the hardware store to arrange for someone to come out to the homestead to replace the smashed window.

Burt Wilson, the town's new odd job man, was delegated to do the job. Burt was relatively new to the town, but his willingness to do any odd job, and do it well, had made him a popular addition to the community.

Harry returned in the company of Sheriff Webster and Zack to find Mary had transformed the inside of the house. In just a few hours, she had scrubbed it from top to bottom and got rid of the water. Only the broken windows and a slight smell of smoke remained, but the charred outhouse roof indicated the ferocity of the raid.

Ben Webster dismounted and began to look round, jotting down a few notes as he did so. Zack, on the other hand, remained on his horse. He spoke a few words to Mary, but completely ignored Harry. The deputy treated Harry as the hired hand, whose opinions were of no account.

Zack then left to search for tracks of

the raiders. He rode off in the direction of the ridge. The same ridge upon which Luke had noticed the two riders watching the barn burn down, although neither Harry nor Mary had mentioned the incident to anyone.

As the deputy left, a large wagon arrived driven by Burt Wilson. Quick as always to respond to an emergency, the handyman had come to replace the broken windows. While he was measuring up, Doc Evans arrived. The good doctor had heard about the raid and had ridden out to make sure Mary was all right.

While Burt Wilson cut the glass to size and fitted it, Mary served tea. Harry was amazed at how well she coped with the situation. It seemed nothing upset her, and before long she had prepared a meal for them. However, Burt declined the offer. He made the excuse that he had been half-way through a job in town and wanted to return to finish it.

Over the meal, the sheriff told them

about the attack on the other home-stead and the raid on the bank. Ben Webster thought it was unlikely the attacks were connected, but was unable or unwilling to come up with any reason for the raids.

As he fitted the window, Burt Wilson overheard them talking. He could have told them what was behind the raids, but he had his own reasons for not doing so. A popular and ever-reliable odd-job man provided the ideal cover for the real reason he had come to Redrock.

The window completed, Burt packed his tools. Mary paid him and he left, but he did not travel far before he halted his wagon and dismounted. Rifle in hand, he walked to a clump of trees, then hid.

Carefully, Burt aimed at the rear wagon-wheel. The first shot missed but the second smacked into the hub of the wheel. The horses pulling the wagon took no notice and continued to graze. Burt smiled contentedly, knowing he would not miss with his next shot, the only one that really mattered.

After the meal was over, Sheriff Webster left, intending to return to town. Old Doc Evans stayed to give Harry a further examination. As before he could find little physically wrong with Harry.

'We know little enough about the body,' said the doctor, 'and even less about the brain or how it works. All I can suggest is that you keep doing what you're doing. Plenty of exercise and good food, then in the fullness of time, nature may restore your memory.'

'What about all the trouble?' asked Mary. 'Won't that make it worse?'

She tried to keep the anxiety out of her voice and not show her feelings. However, the doctor had known her too long not to see through her deception. He was very fond of Mary, whom he regarded as his adopted daughter. Even so, there was little he could honestly say to reassure her.

'Perhaps, but then again, possibly

not,' he replied kindly. 'It's often said when you're drowning all your past life passes before you. Danger might stimulate the brain into remembering, but I don't recommend it.'

'Well, one thing is for sure; I'm not about to try drowning myself just to get my memory back,' laughed Harry. 'I've seen enough of the Red River in full flood to last me a lifetime.'

The doctor looked across to Mary. Her response indicated that she had not missed the significance of Harry's remarks. It was the first time he had mentioned the Red River, one of the great rivers of Texas. Without realizing it, Harry had remembered another fragment of his past. However, the doctor thought it was not yet time to push Harry further. Instead, he left and returned to Redrock.

Doctor Evans had been travelling for less than twenty minutes when he saw a horse he recognized. It was grazing peacefully near a clump of trees. As he drew closer, he noticed the body of Ben

Webster slumped against one of the trees. He did not need his medical training to realize the sheriff was dead.

He left the body where it was and hurried back to town. After arranging with the undertaker to collect it, he hurried to the mayor's office and waited impatiently for his old friend to finish his business with Colonel Masters. As soon as the colonel had left, the doctor began to tell the mayor about the tragedy.

'Jerry, I can't understand what's going on,' he concluded. 'This used to be a peaceful county, yet within a few days we've had raids on homesteads and the bank. Now our sheriff has been killed. Do you think there's a connection?'

'Seems likely, but I'm damned if I can work out what it is!'

'So what will you do now?'

'Guess I'll have to appoint Zack as sheriff, on a temporary basis at least. He's fast enough with a six-gun to take care of any trouble in town — '

'But not the man to find out what's behind the raids,' interrupted Doctor Evans.

'You're right. Zack shoots before he thinks,' agreed the mayor.

'So will you send for a federal marshal?'

'Not yet, Doc. I have already sent for a man to investigate another problem which may be related in some way to our troubles. Let's see what he comes up with first; perhaps the raids are over.'

But they were not over. In the next few days there were more. Three homesteads were burnt to the ground and their owners killed. Finally, an angry Colonel Masters reported his ranch had been rustled. Then, as suddenly as they had started, the raids stopped.

5

At first, Harry knew nothing about the raids, or the sheriff's death. Rebuilding the outhouse roof and repairing the rest of the damaged ranch fences kept him busy from dawn to dusk. He soon discovered that whatever else he may have been in the past, he had not been a handyman. Unlike his six-gun, which felt as if it was part of him, most of the carpentry tools Mary possessed felt unfamiliar. Yet he learned quickly and Mary was more than satisfied with his work.

That work was interrupted by the arrival of Zack Blake, supposedly to pass on the news of the bank-raid, the attacks on the other homesteads and the death of Ben Webster. Actually, the deputy had been well paid to perform another duty and he began by questioning Harry, on the pretext that he had been one of the last to see the sheriff alive.

'Except for his killer,' said Harry.

'Until you and the other stranger arrived on the scene, we were a peaceful community,' Zack continued menacingly. 'The sheriff was murdered near here; where were you when it happened?'

'He was here with me,' interrupted Mary.

'Here, or out working on the range fences?' asked Zack.

Mary's slight hesitation was all the answer the deputy needed. He smiled triumphantly before continuing.

'So, Harry, or whatever your name is, you don't have an alibi, and I know next to nothing about you. I did hear how your horse broke its leg and you had to shoot it, but I never heard why you came here in the first place, or where you originally came from.'

As Harry had little memory of his past, they were two questions he could not answer. Even if he admitted he was the man the townsfolk had derisively nicknamed 'the Barfly', he knew he would not be believed. After all, Mary had gone to a great deal of trouble to change his appearance to try to convince everyone he was a different person.

Fortunately, he was not required to answer either question. Zack was enjoying his newly assumed authority as acting sheriff far too much to pause for an answer.

'So I'll tell you what I'm going to do, the deputy continued. 'I'm going to check through all the wanted posters in the office. If I find there's one out for you, I'll come gunning. So if you want to save yourself, pack up and be on your way.'

'I do the hiring and firing round here,' snapped Mary.

'Maybe so,' retorted Zack, 'but as soon as I'm officially made sheriff I'll be back. Your man had better be gone by then, or ready to use the six-gun he's carrying.'

Neither Harry nor Mary had any chance to respond. Zack jumped on to his horse and savagely raked the unfortunate beast with the spiky rowels of his Mexican spurs. The animal whinnied in pain, but responded immediately by breaking into a gallop.

Mary looked at Harry helplessly. Tears formed in her eyes as she watched Zack ride swiftly away. She hurried into the house to prevent Harry seeing her tears, but she soon returned. Seemingly back in control of her emotions, she clutched the few dollars she had recently earned from the sale of her eggs and milk.

'Perhaps it would be better if you went,' she said.

'You don't owe me anything,' he said, returning her money. 'If it hadn't been for you taking me in like you did, and then tending to me, God alone knows whether I would have survived.'

'Take the money as a gift from a friend. It's not much, but it will help to tide you over until you find some place else.'

'You want me to go?'

'No, Harry, I don't ever want you to leave.'

She spoke from the heart, without thinking. Afraid she had given too much away, she added hastily, 'Ever since you've been here, you've worked well and I trust you. The right kind of hired help is hard to find, especially for a woman living alone. Even so, with all the bad things that have been happening, the last thing I need is trouble with the law.'

She saw the look of pain cross Harry's face when she referred to him as the hired help. Yet it had to be that way. Far better he believed that was the way she thought of him. If he knew how she really felt, he would never leave. Yet it was too soon for the truth; he was not yet ready. However, her words had not fooled him.

'If you don't want me to go, I'll stay,' he replied firmly.

'But what about Zack?'

'Well, this much I'll promise you. I will not go looking for trouble. I'll even keep out of Zack's way as much as possible, but I won't run away. I can't remember how good I used to be with a six-gun, but I think I'm a match for most. If Zack comes looking for trouble, I guess I'll have to find out the hard way.'

In the event, Harry did not have to. Running Harry out of town was only part of Zack's instructions from Colonel Masters. Getting rid of Luke Donovan was the colonel's priority. As a result, Zack only stopped in Redrock long enough to change to a fresh horse, then he rode on to Jeremiah Grande's spread to get the job done.

Colonel Masters paid Zack to secretly do his dirty work. He wanted rid of both Harry and Luke in case they interfered with his 'grand plan', as he liked to call it, especially as his plans were at a delicate stage, making their secrecy essential. So the colonel did not want any gun-toting strangers around whom he could not control.

Not that Zack knew anything of the colonel's schemes, but he did know Mayor Grande had invited Luke Donovan to stay at his farm, and Zack did not like that at all. Although she had given him no encouragement, he considered Elizabeth to be his girl and did not want Luke anywhere near her.

However, Luke's relationship with Elizabeth had not blossomed during his stay. True, they had ridden together several times, but he had deliberately kept his distance, much to her disappointment. She was only too aware how attractive all the local young men, especially Zack, found her. It was just her bad luck that Luke, the first man who had really interested her, seemed indifferent to her charms. She was used to being the centre of attraction and well practised in the art of fending off the amorous advances of the local young bucks. Elizabeth was also used to getting her own way, so handled Luke's apparent lack of interest badly.

After they had returned from one of their rides, she dashed straight to her bedroom in a fit of pique and remained there until the next meal time. Her mother recognized the symptoms but decided not to interfere. There was much about her headstrong daughter which reminded her of herself when she had been young.

Mrs Grande felt it might be good for Elizabeth to find, as she had once done, someone not prepared to fawn all over her. She had married that man and had never regretted it. Jerry Grande had been a cowboy with a well-deserved reputation as a fast gun when they first met. Whereas she had been, like her daughter now, the only child of wealthy parents who had been only too ready to grant her every wish.

Jerry had always been his own man, and had never pampered her. Nevertheless, a deep love, combined with mutual respect, had grown between them over the years, even if, at first, their relationship had been more than a little stormy.

Mrs Grande hoped her daughter would be as fortunate as she had been in finding the right man. In some ways, Luke Donovan fitted the bill admirably, and it seemed Elizabeth was strongly attracted to him. However, she would need to know a great deal more about this enigmatic Southerner before she encouraged her daughter. She smiled ruefully, no doubt her own mother had once felt the same about Jerry.

Jerry Grande had still not returned from town by the time Zack reached the farm. The lawman lost no time in paying his respects to Mrs Grande, and in trying to ingratiate himself with Elizabeth. As usual, she gave him little encouragement. Highly annoyed at her coldness, and the way she looked at the stranger, Zack decided to take his wrath out on Luke and do Colonel Masters' bidding at the same time.

At first Luke did not respond, but he recognized the signs. It was clear the deputy was intent on calling him out. Well, he was not the first. As a successful bounty-hunter, Luke had gained a reputation as a fast gun, but in most towns there was usually someone who wanted to prove they were even faster. None of them had lived to tell the tale.

'I'll say it again,' said Zack, 'I don't want Southern scum in my town.'

'Don't do it,' Luke said calmly, 'you haven't a prayer against me and I don't want a gunfight in front of the ladies.'

Mrs Grande glanced at her white-faced daughter. She took her arm, then squeezed it reassuringly. There was nothing they could do to prevent the gun-play if Zack continued antagonizing Luke.

'Scared?' scoffed the deputy, mistaking the reason for Luke's reluctance to face him. 'Well, I suppose it takes a real man to use a six-gun.'

'Perhaps, but I see no profit in killing a fool,' replied Luke.

The deputy smiled, then without warning, his right hand moved for his gun. He was fast, deadly accurate and supremely confident. Had he not easily outdrawn the four who had gone against him?

In contrast, Luke's hand hardly seemed to move, so smooth was his draw. Like magic, the short-barrelled Remington cleared Luke's holster and spat its message of death towards the deputy. Although the lawman had drawn first, he was dead before his gun cleared leather, the smile frozen on his face.

'I am truly sorry you had to witness that,' said Luke, shaking his head in sorrow as he holstered his Remington.

'Don't apologize,' said Elizabeth. 'He had it coming. I'm just glad it isn't you lying dead on the floor. You're worth ten of him or any other man I've ever met.'

Her face turned crimson with embarrassment, then she rushed into the farmhouse. Luke's eyes followed her, and Mrs Grande saw the sadness in his eyes. It was instantly replaced by a look of concern as the stable boy came running, attracted by the gunshots. Although barely fifteen, Paul carried an ancient but fully primed Springfield rifle-musket. However, when he saw Zack lying on the ground, he stopped and smiled warmly at Luke.

Paul helped Luke to drag the deputy's body over to his horse and draped it across its saddle. As they did so, Mrs Grande hurried into the house and scribbled a note to her husband. She returned immediately and gave the note to Paul. The lad mounted his pony and led the deputy's horse, with Zack's body still draped across its saddle, slowly back to Redrock.

Much to Luke's surprise, Mrs Grande took him by the arm and led him into the kitchen. She insisted he sat down, then made a pot of coffee. Elizabeth came into the kitchen and helped herself to a cup, glancing furtively at Luke as she drank it. Each time she did so, she looked away to prevent Luke noticing, yet she was still upset when he didn't.

If Luke failed to notice, Mrs Grande certainly didn't. She frowned as Elizabeth became more distressed, then nodded her head almost imperceptibly towards the door. Elizabeth opened her mouth as if to protest, but thought better of it as her mother's frown deepened. Instead, she put down her cup and left the kitchen without speaking.

As she left, Luke turned and started to call after her, but he too changed his mind and said nothing. Mrs Grande saw the look of hopelessness in his eyes and decided it was time to become a meddling mother.

'Luke, I think we need to have a talk about you and my daughter,' she said firmly.

'Yes, ma'am, but there's not much to talk about.'

'Oh, but I think there is, young man. I've seen how you look at her.'

'But I've never said anything that might . . . '

He struggled to find the words to express his feelings and explain the situation. Mrs Grande came to his aid.

'I'm not suggesting you have done anything improper, but nevertheless you have had quite an effect on my daughter.'

'I hadn't noticed,' Luke replied ruefully. 'Anyway, after what's just happened, I think it better that I leave.'

'You will do no such thing. Zack drew first. I agree with what my daughter said, even if I might have expressed myself a little differently. Besides, my husband still wants to see you.'

She smiled in an attempt to break the tension. As she had correctly surmised, Luke had misunderstood her intentions. She only wanted to get to know a little more about him, not to prevent him seeing Elizabeth. Her daughter was perfectly capable of running her own life, even if a little unsolicited help from her mother came in handy from time to time.

She thought it was more than possible Luke might be the right man for her daughter. Her only concern was whether he would be able to settle down in the normally sleepy town of Redrock. Or would he become restless and ride away one day leaving Elizabeth with a broken heart? It was going to require all her experience to find out without seeming to be interfering.

Luke sensed the warmth behind Mrs Grande's smile, yet it only made him more determined to leave. His presence had already provoked gunplay, as it nearly always did wherever he went. No, he could not think of subjecting Elizabeth to such dangers. He had chosen to be a bounty-hunter, so leaving Redrock and Elizabeth far behind when the job was over was the price he had to pay.

As if reading his thoughts, Mrs Grande placed a restraining hand on his shoulder. Her eyes betrayed the concern she felt.

'All I need to know about you is that you are not already married, and you will not make any promises to my daughter you know you cannot keep.'

'No, I'm not married, my current occupation makes that out of the question. As to Elizabeth, you have my word I won't mislead her. After this job is over I will move on to the next assignment, that's how I earn my living.'

He had deliberately given Mrs Grande the chance to ask him about the type of work he did. Much to his surprise she didn't, so he concluded his reply had satisfied her and she was no longer worried about him getting involved with Elizabeth. He was right on both counts, but for quite the wrong reasons.

Next day, Jeremiah Grande returned. Far from being disturbed by the shooting, he was secretly delighted Luke had been able to outdraw Zack, whom he had neither liked nor trusted.

'I was afraid you might decide to leave us before I had a chance to put a proposition to you,' he said to Luke.

The mayor ushered Luke into a small room which was usually kept locked. As he entered, Luke saw why. On its oak-panelled walls hung a host of weapons.

Over the fireplace hung two superb and rare Henry rifles. Only a few had seen action during the Civil War, even though they had proved to be the best repeating rifles used in that bloody conflict. On one of the other walls hung a Sharps repeating rifle, a shotgun, several Cavalry sabres and even a cutlass. Locked away in a glass-fronted cabinet was a matching pair of Navy Colts, two of the larger calibre Army Colts and a massive Dragoon Colt.

The mayor paused to pour himself a drink and offered Luke one. He went to a small bureau, unlocked it and pulled out a bundle of letters. He gave a few of them to Luke to read. They all contained offers to purchase various homesteads situated around Redrock. The letters also contained threats of violence against the homesteaders if the offers were turned down.

'So you see, these were not random attacks, but part of a co-ordinated plan,' said the mayor. 'I believe Ben Webster was close to discovering the purpose behind them when he was murdered. He was a much better law-officer than he appeared to be.'

'All this has happened since I arrived here, so it couldn't be the reason you sent for me,' said Luke.

'No, it wasn't. I wanted you to track down a man who rode for Quantrill. Unfortunately, his description is so vague, it could fit almost anybody. However, there is no doubt the man is in the area, but he must wait. I have another proposition to put to you.'

'Which is?' asked Luke.

'To finish the job Ben Webster started. I want you to find out who and why someone suddenly wants to buy land round here. Find him and you may find he is the person organizing the raids.'

'Well, it's a little outside my usual line of work,' said Luke doubtfully. 'Besides, I would need some reason to go poking my nose into other people's business.'

'Not if you were our sheriff,' replied Jerry. 'You see, Redrock doesn't have a charter permitting it to appoint a town marshal but by the authority invested in me, I can appoint a sheriff to cover the county.'

The sheer audacity of the idea took Luke's breath away. Yet why not? True, he was a bounty-hunter and as such had often flouted the law, but there were no Wanted posters out for him. The real drawback was financial, since the pay of a sheriff was not enough to allow him to save towards rebuilding his plantation.

'Pay would be eighty dollars a month, plus keep and all the ammunition you need,' continued the mayor. 'There's an office in town and you're welcome to use a room here.'

The pay was reasonably good, but it was still a long way short of his needs. As if reading his mind, Jerry continued:

'Of course, I will continue to pay you a retainer to keep looking out for the man I'm after. After you've caught him, I'll fix it so you get the reward money.'

'What about a deputy?'

'Pick your own man whenever you need one,' replied the mayor.

'Very well, I'll do it, but only on a temporary basis.'

'Splendid; this calls for a celebratory drink.'

'What does, Daddy?' asked Elizabeth, as she entered the study.

'Luke has accepted the job as sheriff and will be based here as well as in town.'

Elizabeth's face portrayed the range of emotions running through her. Secretly she was delighted at the prospect of Luke staying on at the ranch, but alarmed by the dangers involved in the job he had undertaken.

Luke saw her face whiten and mistook the reason for it.

'I'll only be here part of the time,' he said hastily, 'and then only if you and Mrs Grande agree.'

'Of course we do,' said Mrs Grande from the doorway. 'Now do hurry up, dinner is waiting on the table.'

That evening in his room, Luke could not sleep. He was far from certain he had done the right thing in accepting the position of sheriff. He was only too aware the main attraction of the job was the chance to be near Elizabeth. So to take his mind off her, he concentrated on the raids.

First, there had been the offers for the mayor's farm and the homesteads, all of which had been rejected. Three homesteads had been attacked, and their owners killed. Mary Foster's homestead had also been raided, but for some reason the raiders had broken off the attack. So far the Grande's ranch had been left alone.

Luke could find no pattern to the

raids. Then there was the attack on the bank. Was there any connection between it and the raids? He fell asleep trying to sort it out.

While Luke was asleep, the second raid on Redrock's bank occurred. Whether the gang knew about the deaths of the sheriff and Zack, or whether the timing of the raid was just a coincidence, was a matter for conjecture.

What was certain, however, was the total lack of resistance to the raid. As a result, what might have been originally planned as a hit-and-run attack lasted for several hours.

The gang successfully raided the bank, although they only obtained a few hundred dollars. Meeting little resistance, they went to the saloon and stayed there.

Although they terrorized the saloon girls, they left without causing any damage. However, they then went on the rampage, apparently shooting wildly at all the buildings they passed. Before they left town, the gang set fire to the livery stable.

As a result of the raid, Luke was appointed sheriff without any opposition, not even from Colonel Masters. However, the busiest men in town were Burt Wilson and Doc Evans. The handyman received many requests for help as the townsfolk sought to get back to normal. Fortunately, nobody had been killed during the town's occupation, but many had received minor bullet-wounds or injuries from splinters of flying glass.

Unaware of the raid, Mary Foster drove the gig to the store, which was apparently undamaged by the gang, and purchased her usual supplies. She also bought enough ingredients for Harry to make up a large quantity of ammunition, but was forced to use the money from the sale of her eggs and milk. The storekeeper not only refused her credit, but declined to help her take the supplies to her gig.

Luke had already started his first

patrol as sheriff, although he was not entirely happy with the double-barrelled shotgun the town provided for the purpose. Seeing Mary struggling, he crossed the street to help her. She was surprised to see his sheriff's star.

Together they returned to the store, and Luke also noticed that it had not been damaged by the outlaws. The new storekeeper continued to be unhelpful, even though the store was almost empty. Unaware of Zack's death, the storekeeper treated Luke with contempt, mocking him as he helped Mary load the gig.

'I see the new sheriff is making himself useful,' he laughed scornfully. 'I sell goods from this here counter but I don't load them, so if you want the job on a regular basis, it's yours, sheriff, But I guess Mary is offering you something better than money for your trouble. That is, providing you don't mind sharing with the drifter she's shacked up with.'

The storeman laughed at his crude

joke. Mary blushed, but Luke did not reply. He was still a Southern gentleman who had been brought up to protect the good name of a lady. Once, he would have challenged the man to a duel, but now he just pointed his newly acquired shotgun at the ceiling and fired. The buckshot smashed into the many pots and pans hanging from the rafters, causing most of them to crash to the ground.

'You're going to have to answer to the colonel for the damage you've done,' shouted the storekeeper angrily. 'Someone should have told you, Zack runs things around here. He ain't going to like what you've done one bit.'

'The deputy made the mistake of drawing against me. It was his last mistake, but if you still want to speak to him, that can be arranged,' said Luke, cocking the other barrel of his shotgun.

'No, no,' gasped the storekeeper. 'I'll finish loading the gig right away. As for the damage, that's my mistake. It must have been done by the outlaws during the raid.'

After the gig was loaded, Luke escorted Mary to the edge of town. As he did so, he noticed that not all the properties in Main Street had been damaged, and in spite of the length of time the raiders had spent in it, the saloon was also undamaged.

Mary had been surprised by Luke's explosive reaction to the storekeeper's crude joke, but she assumed he needed to assert his authority. The daughter of a colonel, she had become used to death, so was not disturbed by the news of Zack's fate. His death meant there was no need for her to make Harry leave. She urged the pony onwards, impatient to tell Harry the good news.

6

Once again, an uneasy calm befell Redrock as its citizens did their best to get back to normal. Yet most feared there would be more raids, bringing further killings and more destruction. Luke's appointment as sheriff did little to calm frayed nerves.

Apart from being a stranger and responsible for Zack's death, most believed there was little one man could do against the outlaws. Yet Luke was flooded by pleas for protection. Unfortunately, the pleas were divided between the townsfolk demanding he stayed in town to protect them, and the homesteaders who demanded he protect their property.

Then an irate Colonel Masters rode into town and insisted that Luke should organize a posse to find his herd of cattle, which he claimed had been rustled. Next, the saloon girls demanded his presence in the saloon every evening. Although the saloon had not been damaged by the outlaws, its girls threatened to leave town if Luke did not protect them. Their leaving was something the local cowboys and businessmen were not prepared to tolerate, and they too began to harangue Luke.

Then there were the demands to provide extra protection for the bank. Each time the stage arrived, Luke found he was expected to oversee the transfer of its bankbox. Nearly every stage brought masses of correspondence from other lawmen and federal agencies, with which he was expected to deal. Also, each stage seemed to bring a mass of Wanted posters, all of which had to be studied carefully before being filed away.

There was also the jail. Prisoners had to be fed and guarded. Forms relating to the supply of their food, their fines and even their release had to be filled in. Luke had never worked so hard in his life; there simply were not enough hours in the day. Not that the night brought any relief, for no sooner had he settled down to sleep than a prisoner wanted something, or a gunshot would send him scurrying to investigate the incident.

Yet to the casual observer, the town had almost returned to its usual quiet existence. So Elizabeth could not understand why Luke spent so little time at the farm, or why he was so exhausted when he did. Used to having her own way, she was disappointed and annoyed that he paid so little attention to her. She wrongly assumed he was not interested in her, and had found the saloon girls more to his taste. His insistence that this was not so, that his frequent visits to the saloon were simply part of his duties, only infuriated her even more. However, Luke was too tired to argue. Mrs Grande, seeing his state, chastized her husband.

'Jeremiah, you have simply got to find

some help for the boy. Another week and he will be dead on his feet. Poor Elizabeth is out of her mind with worry, and I won't stand for it a minute longer!'

The mayor had no idea why his daughter should be so concerned about a man she hardly knew, or why his wife was so irate. However, long experience in marriage had taught him he was in serious trouble whenever his wife used his full Christian name.

Jerry knew there was no use arguing, or pointing out Luke had the authority to appoint his own deputy. His wife expected him to put matters right. Therefore, there would be no peace on the domestic front until he did so.

His first move was simple enough. The burnt-out livery stable was a shambles and there was still no sign of the burly blacksmith. Perhaps Brad had left for good after being publicly humiliated by Harry. Whatever, there seemed to be little chance of the stables being rebuilt. Indeed, he understood

Colonel Masters was interested in buying the site and developing it for some other purpose.

So John was out of a job. John had run the stables well enough since the blacksmith's disappearance, so had proved he was suitable to help run the jail. As he employed John's younger brother on his farm, Jerry could always send him to see John and get news about Luke. In this way, Jerry hoped to keep his daughter, and therefore his wife, happy. So he rode to Redrock to make the necessary arrangements.

Unaware of the mayor's activities on his behalf, Luke awoke next morning. He had spent a rare night at the Grandes. Refreshed after an undisturbed night, he washed, then made his way to the kitchen.

Elizabeth was up before him and was already making breakfast. It seemed to Luke she was in a better mood than of late. Perhaps it was just the morning sunshine, but her hair seemed more golden, her eyes even brighter blue. She wore a simple white shirt and a long black skirt, the combination of which emphasized the perfection of her figure. Yet it was not just her beauty which attracted him, there was so much more to her than that. But she was not for him, a bounty-hunter, he told himself angrily. Yet the warmth of her smile suggested differently.

They spent the rest of the morning together, laughing, teasing each other, and occasionally buried in deep conversation. They were oblivious to anyone else, content with their own company, as they walked around the farm buildings supposedly collecting eggs. Mrs Grande twice called them in for coffee, but they did not hear her.

Mrs Grande studied them through the kitchen window, walking hand in hand, just as she had done when she first met Jerry. She looked at her daughter intently. Elizabeth had never looked so happy. The smile on Luke's face told its own story. She took hold of Jerry, just returned from Redrock, and clung tightly to him.

'I know, my love. Just like we once were,' he said softly.

'Still are,' she corrected him, kissing him tenderly in full sight of everybody. 'If she gets half as good a man as I got, she will be very lucky.'

'He's got to do better than that,' Jerry growled.

'Then you don't mind if they get together?'

'Hell no! Don't you think he's a bit like I was at his age?'

'More than a bit, husband dear. Why do you think our daughter loves him, even if she hasn't realized it yet?'

The rest of the day seemed to flash by for Luke and too soon it was time to go. Before he left, he took Elizabeth by the hand and pressed it gently. She was disappointed he did not even try to kiss her, but consoled herself with the thought that the presence of her parents probably prevented him from doing so. As yet she had no idea his reserve was due to his past, and the dangers of the profession to which he belonged.

By the time Luke returned to Redrock, John had already tidied the sheriff's office and taken over the jail. There were only two prisoners. James Brig was unable to pay his fine for being drunk and the other, a tinhorn gambler, was waiting to be tried by the circuit judge for cheating at cards. As neither man was dangerous, Luke was only too glad for John to take over, although he was not prepared to give his young deputy any other duties. John was only seventeen, so Luke judged him too inexperienced to handle life-endangering situations.

Although John was a willing and hard worker, he could neither read nor write. Nor was he any good with a six-gun, so Luke gave him his recently acquired shotgun. Its shortened barrels sprayed buckshot over such a wide area, it was really impossible to miss, providing the target was close.

So there was still nobody to cover Luke's back or to help with the masses of paperwork. There was also the need to track down Ben Webster's killer, the outlying homesteads needed protection, and he still had to recover Colonel Masters' missing cattle. Last but not least was the little matter of finding the man who had ridden for Quantrill. He wasn't going to get rich on eighty dollars a month!

Mrs Grande provided the answer to one of his problems during his next brief stay at the Grandes' farm. She had often helped her husband with the farm accounts, and when he had been first elected mayor, she had been the one who had dealt with all the paperwork. Now she offered to do the same for Luke. It was an offer he could not refuse, any more than he could refuse one of the mayor's Henry rifles to replace the shotgun he had given John.

Nor could he refuse the bewitching look Elizabeth gave him as they said their goodbyes. This time they were conveniently alone. Mrs Grande had seen to that. Luke had only meant it to be a chaste kiss, she had only meant to give a friendly response. Neither of them were ready for the world to erupt around them as they clung desperately together and kissed again and again.

Finally, he pulled himself together, mounted Josh and galloped swiftly away. He cursed himself for losing control of his feelings. Elizabeth watched as he rode away, annoyed and frustrated because she had not really known the true extent of her feelings until he kissed her. Now she had to wait until he returned before she could do anything about them.

7

The advent of good weather, fine food and Mary's company brought no improvement to Harry's memory. However, it became clear he had never been a dirt farmer. Odd jobs he could handle; mending range fences seemed familiar to him; he excelled in riding, hunting and tracking. His Colt seemed a natural extension to his hand and he was a crack shot with a rifle, even when on horseback. Yet he could no more plough a straight furrow than fly to the moon and he did not know how or when to plant crops.

Harry just could not cope with basic farm work. As it was the planting season, everything began to fall behind, forcing Mary to hire two farm hands, Len Williams and Danny Bovine. Both proved to be experienced and hard working, capable of handling all the farm work. As they were used to working as a team, there was soon little left for Harry to do. So it was not long before he began to feel he was not pulling his weight. The arrival of Luke with a job offer resolved the problem.

Luke could not find anyone who admitted to knowing Harry before Mary had taken him in. Yet he could not find any Wanted posters on Harry. On the other hand, if Harry had ridden with Quantrill that was only to be expected.

There were no Wanted posters of Jesse James or his brother Frank, the two most notorious outlaws to have ridden with Quantrill. Although they had robbed many banks and trains, few knew what they, or the members of their gang, looked like. Rumour had it that the gang's last raid had gone wrong, forcing the gang to split up and go into hiding. Soon afterwards, Harry had mysteriously appeared at Mary's homestead.

Nevertheless, Luke decided it didn't

matter who or what Harry had been; he needed a deputy. So he rode over to offer Harry the job. To Mary's dismay, Harry accepted without hesitation. Forty dollars a month would enable him to pay his way and stop sponging off Mary. Once sworn in, he felt good, making him wonder whether he had ever been a lawman.

'What I want you to do,' explained Luke, 'is to work on your own. Stay out here and concentrate on finding Colonel Masters' cattle. Let the other homesteaders know you're around, then see if you can organize them to help each other in the event of any further raids. I'll do the same the other side of Redrock, using the mayor's farm as a base.'

'Do you think there will be any more raids?' asked Mary anxiously.

'Yes,' replied Luke. 'Until we discover the reason for them, I think we must assume they will continue.'

'Any other instructions?' asked Harry.

'It's probably too late to find anything useful, but go to the spinney where the sheriff was killed. See if you can dig up anything which might give us a lead as to who killed him. It's a long shot, but I've turned up nothing at all so far.'

'Will do. When do you want me to report in?'

'I don't,' replied Luke. 'No offence intended, but I don't know how good you are. If something blows in Redrock, I won't have time to wet-nurse anybody else, I've already got John Thomas to look after.'

'No offence taken,' said Harry, 'but watch your back. It doesn't matter how fast you are, you can't beat a shot in the back.'

'That's good advice, but remember the only bushwhacking happened near here, so you keep your eyes open. If anything happens to you, Mary will never forgive me.'

Mary blushed, so Luke was certain his chance remark had hit the target.

From her reaction it was clear she cared deeply for Harry. The way he looked at her made it obvious the feeling was returned with interest. Yet Harry chose to ignore her reaction, probably, thought Luke, for the same reasons he had tried to ignore Elizabeth.

Mary broke the awkward silence by insisting Luke stayed for a meal. He declined, but accepted the offer of coffee. If he hoped to discover anything further about Harry, at first he was disappointed. It was not until the conversation turned to firearms that Harry unexpectedly commented about the Henry rifle.

'I remember briefly using a Henry during the Civil War, then I had to give it back. It's the best weapon I ever used. If they had been issued to my men instead of the standard carbine, maybe we wouldn't have lost so many taking that damned bridge.'

'It belongs to the mayor, but you're welcome to borrow it. I guess I've got used to my own carbine. I find its shorter barrel handier, especially carrying it in town.'

Without realizing it, Harry had recalled an important part of his past, but only Mary realized its significance. The Henry had only been used by the Yankees and only in very small numbers. As the daughter of a Yankee colonel, Mary knew the Union had kept detailed records throughout the war, making it possible to trace the few units which had used the Henry. But for her own reasons, she kept the information to herself. In any case, she could not say anything at that moment for fear of letting Luke in on their secret.

Luke, however, was more concerned with the passing of time. He had been so wrapped up in enlisting Harry, he had not realized how late it had become. Although Redrock was normally quiet during the day, business usually picked up after nightfall. Luke was certain John was not capable of handling serious trouble. So he also did not think about Harry's war

140

experience, but made his excuses and rode Josh back to town.

Next day Harry rode to each of the raided homesteads, but found little in the way of clues. On his way to the spot where the sheriff had been ambushed, he began to feel there was something odd about the raids, but couldn't quite figure out what it was.

As was only to be expected, the site of the sheriff's death had been badly disturbed, but Harry could still make out three sets of wagon tracks. The rear wheel of the first set left a wobbly line which he recognised as belonging to the doctor's gig. The second set were much deeper, obviously made by a far heavier wagon. Harry guessed that wagon belonged to the undertaker.

That left the third set of wagon tracks. Harry dismounted and examined them, but there was little to distinguish them from any other wagon. Then he noticed a tiny fragment of wood only a few feet away from a spot where the tracks deepened slightly. He surmised the wagon must have stopped there for some reason. That aroused Harry's suspicions, since it was very close to the spot where the sheriff's body had been found.

There was no proof that the wagon had had anything to do with the death of the sheriff, or even that the shattered fragment of wood had come from the mysterious wagon. But the tiny piece of wood was all he had to show for his first day as a deputy, so he picked it up and put it in his pocket. Then he remounted Goldwind and rode home. It had been a long day.

Next morning, Harry rode out to the homesteads on his side of Redrock which had not been attacked. He met with a less than enthusiastic response to Luke's idea that the homesteads should join together to provide a force strong enough to deter the raiders. Apart from a natural suspicion of himself and Luke, as newcomers to the county, the remaining homesteaders were all naturally reluctant to leave their own homes unguarded. So Harry gave up on the idea.

It was on his way home that the pattern of the raids became clearer. During the day he had visited several homesteads. He noticed the raided homesteads formed a narrow belt of land running in a straight line northeast from Redrock. All of the unmolested homesteads lay on one side or the other of this belt of land. The only homestead still standing within the belt belonged to Mary, and it had already been raided twice.

Yet what was the significance of the belt of land? Harry pondered the question on the way back to the homestead he now regarded as home. To all appearances, the belt seemed to consist of good farming land. Yet it seemed little different from the rest of the land on each side of it.

Since most of the belt of farm land had been cultivated for many years, any deposits of gold or silver would surely have been discovered long ago. So what made the land worth killing for? Harry did not have the answer as yet, but he had an idea. Maybe the direction in which the belt ran was more significant than the actual land itself.

Sore from two days of hard riding, Harry could not sleep that night. Something other than the mystery of the belt of land bothered him. Something he had seen on his travels was wrong. For what seemed hours, he tossed and turned as he tried to work out what it was. He needed a stiff drink, the craving suddenly hit him hard.

Then, as suddenly as it had come, the craving was gone and he knew what was wrong. It wasn't something he had seen, but what he had not seen. For two days he had ridden all over the northern part of the county without seeing a single sign of the herd supposedly rustled from Colonel Masters. Yet to reach the cattle towns of Dodge or Abilene, the herd would have to travel north through the area he had just crossed.

The only explanation was the herd had not been rustled at all. So why, then, had the colonel reported it missing? He must have known his story would have been checked out. Perhaps that was why Ben Webster had been murdered. But he still had no explanation for the disappearance of the herd.

Although it was some hours before dawn, he got out of bed, dressed and made his way quietly to the kitchen. Over the dying embers of the fire he made coffee, then cleaned and loaded the mayor's Henry. By the time he had finished his second mug of coffee, he had formed a theory. If he was right, he knew the reason for the raids. However, having a theory was one thing; proving it was a different matter. So he decided to keep his theory to himself.

If he had been able to sleep, he might not have heard the raiders. Even then, without the Henry rifle, the raid might well have succeeded. As it was, it was the raiders who were taken by surprise.

Harry waited until they almost

reached the house, then flung open the front door. From a prone position, and at point-blank range, he opened fire. The Henry poured a deadly hail of bullets into the raiders as they galloped headlong into it.

Three raiders crashed to the ground and Harry hit at least one more before the Henry was empty. He threw it back into the house. Still in a prone position, he drew his Navy Colt. As the raiders came to a halt, he emptied the .38 calibre six-gun into them. One more raider fell to the ground.

The raiders returned Harry's fire, but the bullets passed harmlessly over his head. As soon as his six-gun was empty, he pushed the door shut, leapt up and bolted it. Bullets thudded into the closed door. However, the door was hewn from solid oak, so the bullets failed to penetrate it.

Harry began to reload. One of the Henry's other advantages was that it was a breech-loader and therefore loading could be completed in a fraction of the time of a muzzle-loading rifle-musket. By the time the raiders had regrouped, he was almost ready for them.

He was distracted by the arrival of Mary, who had been awakened by the attack. She quickly sized up the situation and began loading his Colt. It was clear from her expertise it was something she had done many times, and Harry could only marvel at her coolness.

'Keep the gun, I'm going out the back door,' he said.

'You will need it more than me,' she said, thrusting the Colt back into his hands. 'I'll get my carbine. Open the window shutter enough for me to shoot at them. With any luck, they won't realize it's not you shooting until you're clear of the back door.'

Harry knew she was right. Once again, he marvelled at her coolness as he reloaded the Henry, then adjusted his holster. As he did so, Mary fetched her carbine. It was another unusual weapon, a single-shot Gallagher, which broke at the breech like a shotgun. Harry remembered seeing it somewhere before, but a barrage of bullets striking the front door drove the memory from his mind.

Once again the oak door proved impervious to the impact of the bullets, and the shooting stopped. Harry gently eased the window shutter open a fraction. It too was made of oak, and was as solid as the door.

It was still dark outside, so Harry could see very little. A bullet thudded into the wall beside him, the flash from the gun barrel came from the almost rebuilt barn. So what had happened to Mary's newly recruited farm hands, who normally slept in it?

Mary, carbine at the ready, pushed him to one side. Without thinking, he kissed her, then made his way to the back door. As Mary fired, Harry gently pushed the door open, crept out and made his way cautiously towards the back of the barn. At each step he expected to be struck down, but the bullets never came. The raiders were too busy keeping out of Mary's covering fire.

On all fours, Harry crawled towards the barn. Mary stopped firing. Harry assumed she was having difficulties reloading the Gallagher, or had run out of ammunition. Taking advantage of the lull, the raiders left the cover of the barn and began to rush the house. At that instant, the first rays of the morning sun lit the yard, making the raiders visible.

Harry opened fire. At that range, the Henry could hardly miss. Several of the raiders staggered, some falling to the ground as if pole-axed. Taken by surprise, the other raiders turned tail and hastily retreated to the front of the barn. Harry winged at least two of them before the rest reached the cover of the barn doors.

However, the sunlight, which had first illuminated the raiders, now lit up the rest of the yard, revealing Harry. He aimed the Henry at the barn and kept firing until he ran out of ammunition. Exposed as he was, reloading was too dangerous, so he dropped the rifle and raced to the back of the barn.

The direction of his run caught the raiders by surprise. They must have assumed he would head back towards the safety of the house, and they opened fire in that direction. Their mistake gave Harry the time he needed to get to the back of the barn, out of sight of the raiders. Even so, it was desperately close and he felt bullets tug at his clothing as they whistled past him.

Gasping for breath, Harry paused by the solid barn wall. The back of the barn overlooked the open paddock, which offered little cover. His position was desperate. Although the raiders could not see him from the front end of the barn, he could not see them either.

Still gasping for breath, Harry sank down on one knee by the corner of the barn furthest away from the house.

Perhaps Mary could cover the side wall facing the house, thus protecting his back. Yet the slow firing-rate of the single-shot Gallagher made this seem unlikely. By the time she had reloaded it, some of the raiders could have rushed the house. If he moved to prevent that, the rest of them could get behind him by running along the side of the barn furthest from the house. Once that happened, Harry knew he was finished.

He drew his Colt and cocked the trigger. There was nothing left to do but wait in the full knowledge that his life would be over in a few moments. Strangely, he was not afraid.

Suddenly shots came from the front of the barn. Harry whirled round, but he had guessed wrong. None of the raiders had tried to get behind him. Instead, the shooting from the front increased dramatically. Throwing caution aside, he turned and raced round the back of the barn. He raced to the house, but by the time he reached it, the raiders were galloping away.

Puzzled by the surprising departure of the raiders, and worried about Mary, Harry dashed into the house. Therefore, he did not see two riders on the distant ridge turn and follow the raiders. They were the same two who had visited the homestead and offered to buy it.

Once inside the house, Harry found Mary unharmed but very distressed. Lying on the floor was the body of one of the raiders. Beside it lay one of the farmhands, Danny Bovine. Blood oozing from the centre of his chest was slowly spreading across his old white shirt. During the Civil War Harry had witnessed several such scenes, and so knew the farmhand's end was near.

'Have we driven them off?' gasped the stricken man.

'Yes, thanks to you,' said Harry.

'Never shot anyone before, may the Lord forgive me.'

Blood dribbled out of Danny's mouth, causing him to cough. Mary stooped down and gently wiped his mouth. She forced a smile as she replied.

'I'm sure he will. You only did it to save my life.'

Danny did not respond, for Mary was talking to a dead man. She closed his eyes and gently laid his head on to the floor, just as the back door was flung violently open.

It was the other farm hand, Len Williams. Although his shirt was blood-stained, he seemed not to have been badly wounded. Smoke still issued from the barrel of the old Starr double-action six-gun he carried in his left hand. Seeing the body of his friend lying on the floor, he cursed loudly, then instantly apologized to Mary.

Mary busied herself clearing up and making coffee while Harry and Len carried Danny's body outside. They had survived the carnage, many of the raiders would never bother them again. Harry searched the dead bodies and found fifty dollars on each of them, evidently payment for the raid.

It seemed someone wanted the homestead very badly. Harry guessed there had been twenty raiders, so assuming the survivors had received the same as those killed, the raid had cost someone far more than the homestead was worth. So what was the real reason for the raid?

Harry had no qualms in collecting the money from the dead raiders. Len collected their guns and ammunition, then rounded up two stray horses. If and when peace returned, Harry would give most of the money to Mary without telling her where it came from. He thought the less Mary knew about the money being paid out to attack her homestead and possibly to kill her, the better. It never occurred to him that someone also wanted him dead.

The bodies had to be removed, so Len rode to the neighbouring homestead to borrow their old farm wagon. Harry went back into the house. As always, Mary had the situation well under control. While they were drinking coffee, he remembered kissing Mary during the raid, and her response seemed to suggest they had once been close, but how could that be?

He dismissed the idea as wishful thinking on his part. Apart from isolated recollections which made little sense, he still remembered little before finding himself sweeping out the saloon. He remembered only too well the disgusting state he had been in. No woman would have had anything to do with a man in such a state. Yet Mary had gone to a lot of trouble to help him start over again.

The return of Len Williams in an old and dilapidated wagon interrupted Harry's train of thought. However, there was nothing wrong with the four mules pulling it. Len explained he had found the neighbouring spread deserted. Apparently, the Duggans family had pulled out, leaving most of their possessions behind them.

Harry and Len loaded the dead

bodies into the wagon, covering them with some old sheets. Harry tethered Goldwind to the back of the wagon, then drove to town. Driving the mule-hauled wagon came easily to him, as if he had done it many times before. He stopped the wagon at the undertaker's and arranged for him to deal with its grisly cargo. Being a lawman had its advantages, even if there were several forms to be filled in.

He left the wagon at the undertaker's and rode Goldwind to the sheriff's office. However, Luke was out on his rounds, so he accepted the offer of coffee from young John Thomas. Harry had barely taken a sip when he heard gunshots. John picked up his shotgun and made for the door, but Harry, aware of the youngster's inexperience, called him back.

'Stay here and guard the jail. Put the shutters up. Don't let anyone in except Luke or me. Shoot anyone you don't know.'

John looked disappointed, but Harry

had no time to spare the boy's feelings. Although Harry had managed well enough on the homestead using the Henry rifle, he didn't know how he would cope in town. The long barrel of the Henry would restrict his movements too much, so he would have to rely on his six-gun. Only time would tell if he was good enough.

'John, while I'm gone, load as many guns as you can. If there's trouble, we may have to make our stand in here.'

The shooting broke out again. It came from the direction of the bank and sounded like several guns ranged against one, making Harry believe Luke might be in trouble. Even so, he looked outside cautiously. Only when he was satisfied there were no gunmen lurking nearby did he leave the sheriff's office and race to the bank.

As he neared the bank, Harry saw Luke was pinned down behind a water-trough. Two masked gunmen had positioned themselves in doorways on opposite sides of the street. Just out of six-gun range, a third gunman held the reins of a group of horses.

Suddenly, from inside the bank, came a muffled explosion. Its force distracted the members of the gang outside the bank for a split second, all the time Harry needed. Still running, he drew, cocked the Colt and fired in one smooth action. The outlaw nearest the bank was hurled against the bank wall by the impact of the bullet smashing into his chest. He slid down the bank wall, dead before he fell to the ground.

Startled, the other masked outlaw spun round to face Harry. He fired from the hip and missed. In doing so, the outlaw moved fractionally out of the doorway. It was enough for Luke! His bullet struck the outlaw in the temple, killing him instantly.

The third outlaw mounted his horse and frantically drove the ones he had been tending down Main Street. The startled horses bolted, kicking up huge clouds of blinding dust. By the time it subsided, the third outlaw was long gone.

Luke raced into the bank while Harry ran round the back. They were too late. In the confusion, the gang had left by the back door. They were not amateurs. Foreseeing that any threat to their raid would come from the front of the bank, the gang had placed more getaway horses behind it. Those at the front were merely a decoy; the gunmen left guarding them expendable in the event of danger.

Although the bank safe had been blown open by dynamite, the bank carried relatively little money. Split up equally between the gang, each member would have got little more than the amount Harry had taken from the bodies of the men who had raided the homestead. As this was the third raid on the bank, the gang must be after something other than money, but what was it?

Harry walked towards the undertaker's but met his wagon before he was half-way there. The undertaker had heard the shooting and correctly guessed there was more business for him. Harry made the figure two in the air with his right hand, and pointed towards the bank.

'You've brought me more business in one day than I normally get in six months. If you keep on like this, I'll have to expand.'

Still chortling at his own joke, the undertaker whistled his mules onwards. Harry turned and walked back to the sheriff's office. Many men had died today and he had been responsible for most of them, yet he felt no remorse. Had he once been a hired gun, or killer? He could not remember.

By the time Harry reached the sheriff's office, Luke was already there, busily sorting through the dead out-laws' six-guns. Unlike those Harry had collected earlier that day, these were Southern copies of the Colt.

Harry recognized them at once. They had been made by Griswold and

Gunnison. Owing to the shortage of iron in the South during the Civil War, they had brass frames. Although their brass frames were otherwise similar to the genuine Army Colt, their barrels were much larger, as they had been copied from an earlier and much heavier Colt design called the Dragoon.

If, as Harry now believed, he had fought for the Union, why could he remember a six-gun used only by the Confederacy? Had he been a spy? That might explain his coming to Redrock, but if he had been a spy, for which side had he really fought?

Only one thing was clear; the Griswold and Gunnison copy was inferior to the real Colt, even when new, and these six-guns were well worn. They were not the type of weapon a top-flight gunman would use, which seemed to confirm his theory that their late owners had been Southern drifters hired as look-outs by the gang.

Luke put the old six-guns away in a drawer, then helped himself to coffee.

Harry finished the cup he had started before the shooting; it was still hot.

'You arrived at an opportune time,' said Luke. 'How come?'

'Had some unwelcome visitors at the homestead,' replied Harry, and went on to relate the raid.

'Seems I chose the right man for deputy,' said Luke, after Harry finished.

'You shot five men,' gasped John, 'not even Jesse James could have killed more.'

'I only killed because there was no other choice,' replied Harry, disturbed by the look of hero-worship on John's face. 'Anyway, if Luke hadn't given me the Henry I wouldn't be here to tell the tale.'

'But you didn't use it when you went to help the sheriff,' protested John.

'The boy's right,' said Luke, 'not many can draw on the run and hit the target dead centre. Where did you learn to shoot like that?'

'Just a lucky shot,' said Harry. 'I was only trying to get his attention.'

'You certainly did that,' laughed Luke, but he wasn't taken in by Harry's evasiveness.

Luke had little doubt in his ability with a six-gun, but even he could not have matched Harry's draw on the run. It could only have been accomplished after years of practice by an expert gunman. Additionally, the five dead men showed, not merely Harry's ability with a rifle, but his remarkable coolness under fire.

Few men were born with these abilities and they could only have been honed to perfection by experience. As a result, such men normally became very well known, either as lawmen or outlaws. The ten-cents novels of the East were full of the exploits of such men. Yet during the time he had been a bounty hunter, Luke had never heard of Harry.

Luke concluded Harry must be using a false name, possibly because he had ridden with the infamous Quantrill's guerrillas. If so, Luke vowed, only one of them would leave Redrock alive. However, for the time being Luke desperately needed his new deputy, so he said nothing, but hoped events would prove his suspicions wrong.

Harry finished his coffee, then left as soon as he could. Apart from being worried about Mary the hero-worship coming from young John was highly embarrassing. He said nothing to Luke about his theory for the raids, since he had no supporting evidence. However, his failure to find any sign of Colonel Masters' missing herd was all the proof he needed that he was on the right trail.

As Harry rode out of Redrock, he passed Burt Wilson's old wagon parked outside the Parton's homestead. There was no sign of the handyman, but Harry noticed that the rear hub of the wagon had been damaged. A light patch of unweathered wood stood out against the rest of the discoloured old wood.

Harry dismounted and bent down to examine the axle-hub. A small splinter had been gouged out of it. He put his hand into his pocket and drew out the bit of wood he had removed from the scene of Ben Webster's murder. It matched the missing piece almost perfectly. He looked closer at the hub and discovered a bullet lodged in it.

Although the piece of wood came from Burt's wagon, it did not mean the handyman had killed Ben Webster. However, it did prove his wagon had been at the scene of the crime and been shot at. So if Burt Wilson had nothing to hide, why had he not reported the incident?

Harry put the splinter of wood back in his pocket, remounted Goldwind and headed home. On the way back he mulled over the evidence. He had most of the pieces of the puzzle, but still no real proof. Until he had there was little he could do.

It was dark by the time he reached the homestead, but he could see Len Williams standing guard, in spite of his injuries. Unfortunately, the farm hand had chosen to stand in a patch of ground illuminated by the light of the full moon, making him an easy target. Harry resolved to teach Len the art of night fighting. He was certain he had been a professional soldier, although he still had few lucid memories of his past.

He approached Len cautiously. During the Civil War, Harry remembered how many lives had been needlessly thrown away because soldiers had approached their own sentries too suddenly. Strangely, Harry could remember approaching sentries on several different occasions, but his memories were fragmented, like half-forgotten dreams. Sometimes he pictured himself dressed in grey, approaching a huge camp on foot. Yet he could also see himself on horseback, wearing a blue Yankee uniform. He could not make any sense out of the little he could remember. The visions of his past seemed to contradict each other, so as he entered the house, he dismissed them from his mind.

By the time he arose next morning,

Mary had restored order to the homestead. Except for the death of Danny Bovine, it was almost as if the raid had never happened, and as the days passed by, normality began to return.

However, Mary was pleased to see a marked change in Harry. Whether it was the result of the raid, or because Luke had appointed him deputy, she did not know, but Harry's confidence had returned in full. He now wore his six-gun at all times and the slight swagger which had once characterized his stride had returned. The shaggy, hangdog look of the Barfly had completely disappeared. Harry was so changed that Mary thought he was rapidly becoming the confident resourceful leader he had once been. Yet for her own reasons, she kept her knowledge of his past to herself.

8

Ten days after the last raid, Harry stumbled upon the evidence confirming his theory about the raids. He left Mary's homestead early that morning to look for signs of Colonel Masters' herd. Not that he expected to find any, but he had promised Luke he would look in the hills about a day's ride north.

The main trail wound round the hills, but Harry rode straight up into them. He searched the hills without any luck until it was almost dusk. Just as he was thinking of giving up, he came across a canyon almost blocked by a large outcrop of rock in its centre. Harry dismounted and carefully led Goldwind past the rocks. On each side of him towered rocky slopes blocking out the evening sun.

As Harry led Goldwind out of the

gloom into the other half of the canyon, he stopped and gasped with amazement. Down the length of its sunlit floor ran a series of tall poles about fifty yards apart. They stretched down the centre of the canyon, as far as the eye could see. A few feet from the top of each pole was a horizontal piece of wood which made it look as if there was a cross on the top of each pole.

Harry remounted Goldwind and rode up to the nearest pole. As he did so, he noticed the sandy canyon floor was covered in the tracks of many horses. As he reached the first pole, he noticed there were several numbers scrawled on the horizontal piece of wood which formed the cross. He rode to the next and found more numbers. As he continued down the canyon he found each pole had a different set of numbers. The poles continued until he reached the mouth of the canyon where they stopped just out of sight of the trail.

At the last pole, the horse-tracks

stopped. Although there was no sign of living vegetation on the canyon floor, Harry found a number of dried leaves by the last pole. He concluded that someone had used some tree branches to wipe out the tracks between the last pole and the trail, which ran about a mile from the north end of the canyon.

Harry rejoined the trail, then turned back towards Redrock and Mary's homestead. He took the longer route home, down the trail, round the hills. Night was falling and he had no wish to retrace his path in the dark through the narrow gap in the centre of the canyon.

It was long past midnight by the time he reached the homestead. He ate sparingly of the supper Mary had left him, then went straight to bed, too tired to ponder the mystery of the line of poles in the northern half of the canyon. Yet when he awoke he knew what they were, for he had remembered seeing something similar during the Civil War. He also knew the raids would go on unabated in their fury unless he could stop them at their source. He would need a detailed map of Redrock County before he could do that.

Mary insisted he took the day off. Apart from wanting to spend some time with him, she was worried he had been overdoing things. Only a few weeks ago he had been the drunken Barfly. So much had happened since then, she was afraid he might revert back.

Harry, on the other hand, felt fine, but welcomed the chance to spend some time with Mary. So when she suggested a picnic, he readily agreed. In spite of the implications of his discovery, the raiders would need time to reorganize after their unsuccessful attack on the homestead, so Harry felt it was safe to leave Len alone. The farmhand had almost recovered from his wounds.

Mary surprised Harry by riding the pony instead of using the gig. She packed the picnic into an old saddle-bag which bore the initials H.F. As he slung it over Goldwind, the saddle-bag looked and felt familiar, although he could not remember seeing it before.

They rode northwards along the trail, then across the ridge where the two mysterious riders had watched the barn burn down. Suddenly Mary swung away and raced across the open prairie towards a distant clump of trees.

The grass was waist-high and still lush green from the spring rains. Mary's little pony was no match for Goldwind and the mighty stallion easily caught up with it. Mary slowed down when she reached the trees and picked her way slowly through them. Harry followed. The area was strangely familiar, yet he could not remember ever riding through the wood.

Mary picked up a little-used trail and her pony broke out into a canter. The trail emerged from the trees and led them across open ground to a secluded valley, through which ran a rippling stream. They rode alongside it until they came to a place where trees lined its banks. They dismounted and while Harry tended the horses, Mary laid out the picnic.

It was a glorious sunny day, so they sought the shade of the trees. Bird-song filled the air. In their search for insects, silver-sided trout leapt out of the stream, only to fall back, their impact sending circles of ripples across the stream. A few buffalo grazed high above them on the slopes of the valley. They were a pitiful remnant of the mighty herds which once roamed across the prairies.

At first they ate in silence. Harry had the strangest feeling he had been to the valley before. He looked around, but said nothing about his strange feeling, content to soak up the idyllic atmosphere. However, he noticed Mary seemed sad, preoccupied with some private thoughts.

'A penny for your thoughts,' he said.

'The last time I came here was with my husband. We found this valley a long time ago and decided that when the war ended, we would settle as near to it as we could.'

'What happened?'

'He volunteered for a mission and never came back,' she said sadly.

'But you came here, anyway?'

'Yes. You see they never found his body, so I figured if he was still alive, he would find his way back here someday.'

Harry was about to answer when he heard a faint sound. Instinctively his hand reached for his six-gun, but then he relaxed. It was the sound of cattle bellowing in the distance, the noise echoing and distorted by steep valley sides.

'Yes. I heard them too,' said Mary. 'It looks as though someone else has found our valley, although it seems a very isolated place to keep cattle.'

'Unless you wanted to hide them,' said Harry, remembering the herd rustled from Colonel Masters.

Except the herd showed no sign of being rustled. It took him only a few minutes to mount Goldwind, ride down the valley and locate the supposedly missing herd. Several hundred cattle were corralled in a box-canyon at the far end of the valley.

Harry could not see anyone guarding the herd, so he opened the corral gate and rode in. He inspected the brand on about fifty steers and was not surprised to see Colonel Masters' brand had not been changed on any of them. Another piece of the puzzle clicked into place, but there were more facts to be established before he could make any accusations stick.

He rode out of the corral, closing its gate behind him. If he was correct, this valley was no place for a picnic. Even in the seclusion of the trees, Mary might not be safe. However, he slowed down before he reached her, so she would not be alarmed.

Mary had no way of knowing his concern for her safety, nor why he had suddenly left to find the herd. So when he suggested they return to the farm, she assumed he was not enjoying the picnic and so agreed reluctantly. Later that night she broached the subject.

'I'm sorry you didn't enjoy the picnic. The place is special to me, and I wanted to share it with you.'

'But I did like it, and I really appreciate you sharing your special place with me. You know, I had the strangest feelings all day. First I thought I recognized your saddle-bag, and all day I felt as if I was revisiting old haunts.'

Mary's face remained expressionless, despite the feeling of elation which surged through her. Even her voice was perfectly calm as she continued speaking.

'Is that why you wanted to leave?'

'No. The herd is the one Colonel Masters reported missing.'

'Oh! So that's why you wanted to leave so suddenly. You were afraid the rustlers might find us.'

'Something like that.' He didn't tell her there were no rustlers, because none of the herd had been rustled, in spite of what the colonel had claimed. Nor would he say anything to Luke until he had found out why the colonel had lied.

9

After the last raid on the bank, Redrock calmed down beyond all expectations. It was so quiet, there was little need for Luke to continue his evening vigil over the saloon, much to the disappointment of the saloon girls.

As the jail was empty, its only remaining prisoner having been tried and found not guilty by the circuit judge, John Thomas busied himself in the sheriff's office. He was a surprisingly quick learner and eagerly took over the mundane chores and non-dangerous tasks which had initially overloaded Luke to the point of exhaustion.

Mrs Grande had more than kept her word regarding her offer to help out over the paperwork. Apart from organizing a daily cleaner, she regularly came to the office and did most of the paperwork. She also tidied the office, filed the new Wanted posters after Luke had finished studying them, and dealt with the routine correspondence.

Mrs Grande was the model of efficiency, so all Luke had left to do was sign the letters. Indeed, with Harry patrolling the range north of the town, Luke began to enjoy life again and accepted an invitation to stay at the Grandes' farm for a few days.

'After all, we have set up a room for you,' said Mrs Grande, 'and I'm sure my daughter would like to see you again.'

Of course he wanted to see Elizabeth again, but she was the reason he had stayed away from the Grandes' farm. Or to be more exact, his feelings towards her, combined with her passionate response to his kiss, had caused him to stay away. Until he had sufficient money to rebuild his old Southern home, there was no place in his scheme of things for any woman, except an occasional saloon girl to satisfy his normal manly instincts.

It seemed his fears of getting involved were misplaced. His arrival at the Grandes' farm seemed to arouse little enthusiasm from Elizabeth, who appeared to go out of her way to avoid being alone with him. During the first two days, on the rare occasions they met she was chaperoned by her mother. Luke did not know if he was relieved or disappointed.

Not that he had much free time. Jerry Grande returned looking most concerned, and took Luke into his private study. Apparently the mayor had been summoned to the Circle K Ranch where an irate Colonel Masters had harangued him about the way he was running Redrock.

The colonel had made it clear he was unhappy about Luke's appointment as sheriff, arguing he should have been brought to trial over the shooting of Zack. He went on to say he should have been consulted over the appointment of

Harry as deputy and concluded by threatening to stand against the mayor at the next election.

'He would win, too,' concluded Jeremiah Grande.

'How come?' asked Luke.

'As I told you when we first met, the colonel is the main employer around Redrock. Apart from owning the Circle K, he owns the saloon and several other properties in town. Not only has he just bought up the ruined livery stable, but he has also purchased the three derelict homesteads which were attacked by the raiders.'

'What does a big rancher want with three small homesteads?'

'I've no idea,' replied the mayor, 'but he paid cash each time.'

'Does he keep his account in the Redrock bank?'

'I'm not sure, but I don't think so. If he had lost any money because of the raid, I'm sure I would have been the first one he would have blamed.'

Luke left later that evening. Although

there was no moon, the stars seemed to be shining extra brightly, making the well-worn trail to town easy to follow. This time there had been no goodbye kiss from Elizabeth. She had not even bothered to *say* goodbye to him. All for the best, he told himself.

His thoughts were centred on Elizabeth, so for once he was caught unawares when the usually sure-footed Josh stumbled. Luke was almost thrown, so the bullet intended for his heart zinged harmlessly by.

Even so, Luke flung himself to the ground and lay prone as if he had been hit. Because he had been thinking about Elizabeth and not concentrating on the trail, he had not seen the gun flash so he had no idea where his assailant was hiding.

Knowing Josh would not roam far, Luke lay still in the hope his would-be murderer would move closer to finish off the job. Although he remained absolutely still for twenty minutes, nothing happened, although he heard the sounds of a wagon driving slowly away.

He waited until the sounds of the wagon faded away and carefully stood up. Nothing untoward happened, so he whistled for Josh. The big stallion trotted up to him instantly and nuzzled his hair. Luke mounted and rode off after the wagon, but clouds began to cover the stars, so he found no trace of it, and returned to Redrock without further incident.

Next day was Saturday. It was unusually quiet, even the usual cowboys seemed to have decided to give Redrock a miss. That night, the saloon girls heavily outnumbered the paying customers, making Luke think the Circle K hands had been warned to stay away. If so, it hardly made sense, for their boss, Colonel Masters, also owned the saloon. Unless, of course, the Colonel expected another raid, and so was keeping his men out of the way.

Luke was uneasy, so he kept a special look-out for trouble as he made his nightly patrol. Yet all was quiet, too quiet, Luke felt. So, an hour after he had returned to the sheriff's office, he changed into a pair of moccasins and slipped out of the side door. Under the cover of darkness, and using all the back alleys he could, he made his way silently round the town.

An hour later, he returned. In spite of all his precautions he had found nothing untoward. Redrock was as peaceful as a graveyard. Yet his feelings of unease persisted and he slept with his hand next to his six-gun.

Sunday came and went, as quietly and uneventfully as Saturday. The days which followed were equally peaceful, yet Luke's feelings of impending doom grew stronger as each day passed. At last he could stand it no longer, so he rode out to Mary Foster's homestead to exchange news with Harry.

Harry told Luke how he had found the Colonel's missing herd and that none of the brands on the cattle he had examined had been changed. Harry kept his suspicions about the colonel to himself, nor did he say anything about the strange line of poles he had found. But he did tell Luke about finding wagon-tracks at the scene of Sheriff Webster's murder and matching the splinter of wood he had found there to Burt Wilson's wagon.

Luke's eyes narrowed as he recounted his lucky escape from the unknown marksman who had apparently driven away in a wagon. He did not mention that he had been careless because he had been thinking about Elizabeth at the time.

'Of course, we have no real proof that Wilson is the man who killed Ben Webster, or shot at you,' said Harry. 'Can you think of any reason for him doing so?'

'No, I can't,' said Luke, 'but that won't stop me shooting the son of a bitch the first time he steps out of line.'

Luke returned to Redrock. He was surprised to find John Thomas was not alone in his office. Elizabeth was also there. She appeared most agitated.

'Colonel Masters is holding a meeting in the saloon,' she said. 'He's called the most important town members together to try to persuade them to make him mayor and get rid of you as sheriff. He's saying you are really part of the gang which raided the bank and that's why they got away.'

'That's ridiculous. I wasn't appointed until after the raid.'

'Of course it is, but Daddy says the colonel carries a lot of influence and his lackeys outnumber Daddy's friends. He wants you to come home with me until the trouble blows over.'

'I must let Harry know what's happening,' said Luke. 'I got him into this mess, so it's up to me to get him out of it.'

'Couldn't you send John Thomas? Perhaps he could persuade Harry and Mary Foster to stay with us as well.'

Luke nodded his head in agreement. They could always leave Len Williams to look after their homestead. The townsfolk would be unlikely to bother him and the outlaw gang seemed to have stopped operating, for the time being at least.

'Saddle up and be ready to leave when I say,' Luke ordered John.

While John saddled up, Luke collected a spare six-gun, a massive Colt Dragoon and as much spare ammunition as he could carry. Although he normally preferred to make his own, he was grateful that Ben Webster had created a large stockpile.

The problem with using other people's ammunition was you didn't know whether it was reliable. Ammunition had been known to fail, or worse still, backfire, and ignite the other bullets stored in the rest of the six-gun's cylinders. Such a misfire could blow a man's hand to smithereens. However, there was no time to make any more bullets, and he had insufficient of his own to hold off any mob instigated by the colonel.

A perspiring Jeremiah Grande entered

the office. It was clear the debate was not going his way, and he welcomed the glass of whiskey offered to him, in spite of his daughter's disapproving looks.

'Masters has put a proposition to the council, but I have suggested an alternative plan. The council have retired to consider them. Unfortunately, the colonel has the money and the influence to back up his plans, so it doesn't look good. I'm just sorry I got you into this mess.'

'Luke, if you left now, you would be safe,' said Elizabeth.

'I've been in some sort of trouble most of my life,' replied Luke. 'One thing I've found, running away from it does no good.'

'One day, when this is all over and Redrock gets back to normal, I will remind you about what you just said.' Elizabeth blushed deeply as she finished speaking, although Luke did not understand her reason for doing so.

'First, we got to get Redrock back to normal,' he replied. 'Without me that ain't going to happen.'

There was no bravado in his statement. It was a matter of fact, and Jerry Grande recognized it as such. So far the citizens of Redrock County had been on the receiving end of a gang of outlaws. Whether they realized it or not, they had to fight back. The mayor was certain there was nobody better to lead them than Luke and possibly Harry.

For the moment, however, public opinion was on the side of the colonel, so it looked as if he would be able to get rid of them. Actually, it was only that part of the public opinion which could be bought or intimidated, Masters' ranch hands, the tenants who leased his shops and business premises in town, and the saloon girls. Not that they had any direct say in the council's affairs, but they threatened to tell the wives of those council members who regularly availed themselves of the services the girls provided in the saloon's notorious bedrooms.

In the event, not everyone succumbed to the various pressures used by the colonel. As a result, the council were deadlocked, as Jerry discovered when he returned. The argument raged on into the small hours of the morning, until finally a compromise was reached. A compromise the furious Colonel Masters was forced to accept, with as much good grace as he could muster. For the moment his good public image was all-important to his plans.

Luke and Elizabeth did not wait for the meeting to end. Luke was concerned about Elizabeth's safety in the event of the colonel gaining the upper hand at the meeting, and his cronies attempting to remove him from office by force. There was no other way Luke was going to give up the badge, until he felt the time was right for him to do so.

Remembering how he had recently been ambushed, he insisted that Elizabeth ride home on her own. Luke felt she would be safer riding alone, for there was no reason for his would-be assassin to associate her with himself. Besides, with Elizabeth out of the way and most of the town not actually involved in the meeting, drinking free beer in the saloon, it was an ideal chance to do some snooping. Perhaps he could find out a little more about Burt Wilson.

Even from the sheriff's office, Elizabeth could hear the sound of revelry and raised voices coming from the saloon. Since the free beer was being donated by Colonel Masters, she guessed his lackeys were baiting the crowd against Luke. So she was not happy about him being alone in Redrock, and only agreed to go on his promise that he would not stay longer than was absolutely necessary.

'Josh is much faster than my pony, so if you're not at the farm within an hour of my arrival, I'll head straight back. You had better believe me,' she said angrily.

He did, although he had no idea why she was so angry with him. As she was leaving, he loaded the ammunition into his saddle-bags. They were heavy.

As soon as Elizabeth was out of sight, he checked his six-gun and stuck the old Dragoon in his belt. The big old Colt had a kick like a mule, but it carried a much heavier punch than the .36 calibre Navy Colt he normally used. Finally, he picked up his Spencer carbine and walked out of the office. He made no attempt to shut the door, as he did not expect to be using the office again.

As he had hoped, the streets were empty. Those not imbibing the free drinks in the saloon had stayed indoors, safe behind shuttered windows. They were right to do so, thought Luke, for he had seen the signs many times before. Otherwise decent citizens, once liquored up, could be rapidly turned into a lynch-crazy mob by the inflammatory words of a few well-placed men.

Burt Wilson had a small cabin at the back of town. The area had been set aside to house the saloon whores, most of the properties belonging to Colonel Masters. As the saloon was doing record business, it came as no surprise to Luke to find the area completely deserted.

He dismounted near to Wilson's cabin. There was no sign of life, and despite the gloom of the early evening sky, no light came from the cabin's interior. The door was not locked, so Luke drew his Navy Colt and entered cautiously.

His caution was unnecessary. The cabin was empty. For a man supposedly living on his own, the interior was surprisingly clean and tidy. In the kitchen, pots and pans glinted and gleamed in the flickering light of a recently made-up fire. The bedroom was immaculate, dusted and polished. The single bed had been made up with freshly laundered linen.

Luke carefully opened a bureau beside the bed and went through its drawers. He found Wilson's clothes neatly folded away, freshly laundered and ironed. In the wardrobe he found not clothes, but a small arsenal of guns and ammunition. Clearly there was more to Burt Wilson than met the eye. He was not just an ordinary handyman.

One of the bureau's doors was locked. However, it was a cheap lock, and Luke had little difficulty prising it open with a knife he found in the kitchen. The drawer contained numerous cuttings from old newspapers, all lauding the exploits of Quantrill's notorious guerrillas. Under the cuttings was a letter from the Western and Central Railroad Company.

Josh's neighing warned Luke of approaching horses. There was neither time to read the letter, nor repair the drawer-lock, so Luke stuffed the letter inside his shirt and left the cabin as silently as he had entered it. He mounted Josh and rode swiftly away, more to beat Elizabeth's deadline than to avoid the two riders approaching Wilson's cabin.

He need not have worried in either

case. The two riders started to chase Luke, but their small Texas ponies, though nimble, were no match for Josh. The mighty stallion easily outpaced them, leaving their riders choking in his dust. Josh had little difficulty in maintaining the brisk pace, even with the additional weight of the ammunition in the saddlebags, and they arrived at the Grandes' farm only a few minutes after Elizabeth.

10

The council debated until the early hours of the morning. Finally, a compromise deal, acceptable to Colonel Masters, was thrashed out. Mayor Grande was far from happy with the deal, but it was the best his few friends left on the Council could negotiate. In any case, when the time was right, Jerry had a few aces left to play.

Having thanked his friends, Jerry, now the ex-mayor of Redrock, hurried to his office and collected his personal belongings. In spite of the late hour, celebrations were still under way in the saloon, so Jerry thought it prudent to leave at once before they got out of hand. He arrived at his farm at sunrise, so went to bed without telling his wife about the sacrifice he had just made.

A few hours later, Mary Foster and Harry rode up to the farm. They were accompanied by John Thomas driving a wagon, into which Mary had packed her most treasured possessions. They were greeted warmly by Mrs Grande, although she knew nothing of the events causing their arrival. She insisted they ate breakfast while Elizabeth supervised the unloading of their wagon.

While they ate breakfast, Mrs Grande worked feverishly to reorganize the farmhouse. Mary was to share Elizabeth's room, while Harry and Luke were moved into the spare room. John moved into the bunkhouse with his brother and the two other farmhands. They only worked on the farm during the busy planting season, and at harvest time. Both were ex-army men who had fought during the Civil War for the Union.

It all took time to organize, but by the time Jerry awakened, his wife had completed the reorganization. Jerry had intended to discuss the situation with only Luke and Harry, but the women were determined not to be left out.

Recognizing that the normal way of life on the farm had been severely disrupted, Jerry gave way, including everyone except the farmhands in the discussion. Normal farm work still had to be done, and the need to keep a constant vigil was of paramount importance. John Thomas was given the task of arranging the look-outs.

It was mid-afternoon before the meeting eventually got under way in the main living room. They sat around the dining table and began to help themselves to the large pot of coffee Mrs Grande had made.

'As some of you know,' began Jerry, 'last night there was an emergency meeting of the town council, called by Colonel Masters.'

'For what reason?' asked Mary.

'To discuss the bank raids and the attacks on the homesteads. In effect it was a vote of no confidence in the way I had been running matters,' said Jerry.

'But you appointed Luke as sheriff

and made Harry deputy,' said Mary.

'And made John Thomas a sort of deputy,' interrupted Elizabeth.

'Plus agreeing to Mrs Grande acting as my unpaid secretary.' added Luke.

'We really haven't had that much time to do anything,' said Harry. 'Unfortunately, thorough investigations can't be completed overnight.'

'What does Colonel Masters hope to gain by getting the council to vote you out of office?' asked Mrs Grande.

'The Colonel wants his own men running the town.'

'But that's not fair, Daddy,' said Elizabeth, 'not after all the work you've put in.'

'I guess the Colonel has his reasons,' said Luke.

'Yes. Unfortunately, having no news about his herd strengthened his case. Apparently Masters has been unable to fulfil his contract with his buyer in Abilene because of the amount of cattle rustled. The council were also unhappy about the lack of progress in finding the murderer of Ben Webster. It seems the colonel had unofficially appointed Zack as Webster's replacement, although nobody on the council had seen fit to consult me. When Luke outdrew him and I appointed Luke as sheriff, I'm told the colonel was furious.'

'So what actually happened last night?' asked Elizabeth.

'Well, I'm no longer town mayor. Worse still, Luke and Harry have been dismissed by the town council,' her father replied.

A gasp of dismay went round the room. Harry was about to say something, then changed his mind. He would wait and find out what the others had to say before he outlined his theory behind the raids.

Luke also said nothing, but he was not too disappointed about losing his status as sheriff. Now he could go after Burt Wilson without the need to provide the court with evidence of the man's guilt. Additionally, if he was to revert to being just a bounty-hunter, he could spend more time looking for the man who had ridden with Quantrill, the original reason he had been summoned to Redrock.

'So what happens now?' asked Mrs Grande.

'Well, I may have lost control of the town, but the town doesn't control the county,' replied Jerry, grinning mischievously.

'And your appointment is by the county,' said Mrs Grande, half guessing what her husband was going to say next.

'From the Governor himself,' laughed Jerry. 'I've already written to him telling him about the situation. Young Paul can meet the stage with it tomorrow. I guess we had better stay out of town for the moment, since Masters has already appointed a new law-officer.'

'Surely that's not legal!' said Harry. 'I seem to remember a town has to have a charter before it can appoint its own law-officer.'

'Quite right, but it's something of a technicality,' replied Jerry. 'As I said, I've written to the Governor about the situation, but I don't expect immediate action.'

'Why not?' asked Elizabeth.

'It's not likely there will be many complaints about the way the law will be enforced in town. Masters and his henchmen will see to that. So it's possible the Governor will wait to see how things work out before doing anything. Of course, he will institute an investigation eventually, but that could be several months away.'

Jerry shrugged his shoulders, then helped himself to a mug of coffee. His wife disappeared into the kitchen and returned with a tray of hot buttered scones.

'So what happens now?' asked Luke, after they had finished eating.

'You and Harry remain the official county law-officers,' replied Jerry. 'One of your new duties will be to ensure that the town's new marshal, to give the man his correct title, does not attempt to extend his jurisdiction outside the town limits.

'So who is the new town marshal?' asked Harry.

'Burt Wilson,' came the astounding reply.

For a moment nobody spoke. Luke alone was not surprised. He reached into his shirt and pulled out the letter he had taken from the cabin of the new town marshal. A look of pure innocence came over his face, as he broke the silence.

'I took the liberty of calling on our new marshal, last night. Unfortunately, when I got there, he wasn't in. So I started to read this letter while I was waiting for him. I guess I must have put it in my pocket and forgot about it.'

Luke's face was a picture of innocence, as he gave the letter to Jerry. The ex-mayor read it slowly, then read it again, as if he could not believe its contents.

'It's from the Western Central Railroad,' said Jerry. 'The letter authorizes the holder to act as their agent.'

'So why would Wilson have it?' asked Mary.

'I think I can answer that, and the reason for the raids,' said Harry.

'How come?' asked Luke.

'Well, first I have to admit to not passing on all the information I've gathered since I was appointed deputy. You see, before I started to make any accusations I needed to find more proof.'

'How so?' asked Jerry.

'I needed a reason to explain the missing herd, and a motive for anyone killing Sheriff Webster.'

'But Harry, I don't see how the letter helps,' said Mrs Grande.

'Before I answer that, let me ask if anyone here has ever heard of the Western Central Railroad?'

No one had. Mary looked at Harry in amazement. He was so confident, all trace of doubt gone. Had he finally buried his experience as the Barfly, and returned to his old self? For a second she thought he had, but her hopes were soon dashed.

'I have to confess to some loss of memory due to the Civil War. However, I do remember coming across the Western Central. Only in those days it really acted as an information-gathering organization.'

'You mean it was a company of secret agents? Which side did they work for?' asked Elizabeth.

'Both. I believe originally the company owned a stage-coach line. Then it took over two small railroads that went bust. One operated in the South and the other in the North. During the Civil War both lines carried troopers and agents, who befriended any of them gullible enough to talk about their war experiences.

'Played both sides against each other,' said Luke grimly.

'How? I don't understand,' said Elizabeth.

'Harry means the northern part of the railroad spied on the Union, then sold the information it gathered to the South. At the same time, the southern part of the railroad spied on the Confederacy, then sold its information to the Union,' said Mary Foster.

'But what's this got to do with all the terrible things that have been happening in and around Redrock?' asked Mrs Grande.

'Everything. You see, this railroad is the cause of all our troubles,' replied Harry.

'You're going to have to explain that to me as well,' said Jerry.

'Somehow, this railroad must have survived the war, and now it's looking to expand,' said Harry.

'But what's this all got to do with Ben Webster's murder, or the missing herd?' asked Mrs Grande.

'I'll come to that,' said Harry. 'You see, I found three clues, but until the letter, I hadn't a motive to link them together.'

'What clues?' asked Jerry.

'The first was a splinter of wood, which Luke and I agreed put Burt Wilson's cart at the spot where the sheriff was murdered. I also suspected him of being responsible for the attempted ambush of Luke the other night.'

'Luke, you didn't tell me,' said Elizabeth, accusingly. The look of near-panic on her face betrayed her innermost feelings. Her mother and Mary exchanged knowing looks, yet the men noticed nothing unusual.

'The second clue came when I found Colonel Masters' herd,' continued Harry.

'I didn't know you had,' interrupted Jerry. 'It might have helped a bit last night, if I could have told the colonel where it was!'

'He knows,' said Harry. 'I found them in a box-canyon when Mary and I went on a picnic. The herd is safely corralled and being well looked after. Indeed, somebody has been feeding them regularly. Yet oddly, not one brand had been changed.'

'Very odd,' said Jerry. 'You would think that would be the first thing any rustlers would do. But what had the colonel to gain by saying his cattle had been rustled?'

'Until just now, that's what I couldn't figure out,' said Harry, 'even though I had already come across a line of marker-poles to the north of the three homesteads destroyed in the raids. I ought to have realized what was going on when the colonel complained about not being able to complete his deal with the cattle-buyer in Abilene. I couldn't put it together until Luke found the letter. Its contents should be enough to hang Masters and Wilson.'

'But I don't see how,' protested Jerry.

'Me neither,' admitted Luke.

'The three homesteads ransacked by the outlaw gang and bought up by Masters all lie in a straight line, due north. Extend that line and you come to the markers I found.'

'You mean it's a possible railroad route into Redrock!' exclaimed Luke, at last realizing what Harry was getting at.

'Yes. I think Sheriff Webster found the markers and told Zack about them,' said Harry.

'Zack then passed the information to Colonel Masters,' said Luke.

' . . . who in turn told the railroad's undercover agent, Burt Wilson, to kill Sheriff Webster, to stop the news getting out,' concluded Harry.

'That all makes sense up to a point,' said Mary. 'But why the raids, and what's Colonel Masters' herd got to do with it, rustled or not.'

'Land values always rocket when railroads want to buy,' said Jerry, 'and Masters has bought up the homesteads and the livery stable for a song. But I have to admit I can't see where the herd comes in.'

'Masters had a deal with a cattle-buyer in Abilene,' Harry continued, 'but it's a hard trail, and along the way there are bound to be losses. Then there's

Indians to trade with, and farmers' lands to be crossed. The farmers near Abilene charge tolls for the right to cross their land. How much easier and more profitable to sell them to the railroad, if one came to Redrock.'

'Especially if you owned some derelict land in town, suitable to turn into cattle pens, or even a station,' said Jerry.

'Of course! The livery stables,' said Mary Foster, remembering it was there that Harry had come to her rescue. She blushed as she remembered how the blacksmith had tried to rape her, and how Harry had thrashed the vile man, even though Harry was terribly weak and Brad was almost twice his size and weight.

'Well, it all makes sense at last,' said Mrs Grande.

'Yes, but making it stick in a court of law is another matter,' said Luke. 'Remember, Masters runs the town and the law there.'

'So we set a trap and catch the gang when it next strikes,' said Harry. 'That should force Masters out into the open.'

'If we can take a couple of the gang alive, maybe they can be persuaded to talk. We could hold them here until the circuit judge comes,' said Jerry.

'But there's far too many of them,' said Mary. 'We were lucky to survive the last raid.'

'That's because we weren't ready for them,' said Harry. 'Masters has become greedy. I'm betting he will try again for your homestead, Mary. This time we will be ready and I'll have Luke, young John and Len Williams in prime positions, waiting for them.'

'But that's only four against twenty or more,' protested Mary.

'Five counting me,' said Jerry. 'It's some time since I handled a six-gun but I used to be pretty good, and I'm still pretty good with my Henry.'

Luke looked at the portly ex-mayor of Redrock doubtfully, then across to Harry. He saw the same look of concern spread across his deputy's face.

Whatever he had once been, Jeremiah Grande might prove to be a greater liability than an asset. However, there was no doubting the man's courage, and the last thing Luke wanted to do was to put him down in front of his family.

Mrs Grande excused herself and left the room. She returned with a gun-belt and holster containing a pearl-handled Navy Colt. She gave it to her husband.

'Let's see what you can still do, darling,' she said, smiling at her husband. 'I think it's time you showed our daughter the other side of the man I married.'

Jerry buckled on the gun-belt and they all followed him outside. Luke set up a line of tin cans in groups of three on the corral fence. He paced out twenty steps, turned and fired in one motion, sending each of the three tins in the first group spinning away into the air.

Harry moved to Luke's side. He drew and fired from the waist without seeming to take aim. Nevertheless, he hit all three tins in the second pipe dead centre.

Finally, it was Jerry's turn. In spite of his outward appearance of calm, his wife was anxious, hoping she had not placed her husband in a position where he was going to make a fool of himself.

Jerry's draw was surprisingly quick for a man well over forty. There was little trace of rust as his right hand closed on the pearl-handled Colt. His draw was as smooth as silk, cocking the six-gun as he took aim. Indeed, he was only a little slower than Harry, but only two of the three tins went spinning into the air.

Nevertheless, it was a remarkable performance from a man who had not drawn a six-gun for many years. Although he served during the Civil War, he had been offered, and had accepted, a staff commission. Texan by birth, he had fought with distinction during the Texas War of Independence. Yet he detested slavery, so he had fought for the Union.

To prove his shooting had not been a fluke, Jerry restacked the tins. This time they all stood shoulder to shoulder, and drew simultaneously. Luke's was the first tin to fly into the air, but it was only a fraction ahead of Jerry's. Although Harry's first tin was the last to leap into the air, there was little in it. Shooting from the waist, he was the first to get all three shots off, using his left hand in a fanning motion to cock the six-gun before each shot.

'Where did you learn that trick?' asked Luke.

'Around,' said Harry vaguely, not wishing to admit he could not remember. 'But what about Jerry then? Think how fast he must have been in his younger days.'

'None quicker,' said Mrs Grande proudly, and continuing in a voice loud enough to ensure her daughter could hear, 'Jerry was the top gunfighter around when I first met him.'

The exhibition over, they moved back

inside. There were tactics to discuss, plans to be made. Mrs Grande excused herself and went to make tea. Presently her daughter joined her, a troubled look marring her pretty face.

'Mother, how did you meet father?'

'Does that really matter, dear?'

'No, but weren't you scared because he was a gunman?'

'No more than I am now.'

'I don't understand?'

'Of course not, dear. You see, I saw there was more to your father than just being a gunfighter. I thought, with a little help he could change.'

'And he did, didn't he?'

'Not really, darling. Yes, he kept his promise and never wore a six-gun after we married. But deep inside, he's never really changed. I was wrong to try to alter him, so I gave him back his six-gun.'

'But aren't you scared, Mother?'

'Yes, dear, but I still wouldn't have your father any other way. You see, he's tried so hard over the years to make a good life for us. To sit around while someone tried to take it away from us would have taken away what's left of his pride, even if Luke and Harry won.'

'Mother, I'm so frightened.'

'For your father, or for Luke?'

'Both!'

'Then I suggest you tell your father how you feel. If you're sure of your feelings for Luke, you had better find some way to show him when you're next alone with him.'

'Mother! How could you suggest such a thing?'

'Nonsense, child. Luke has to know the way you feel. Otherwise, he will ride away when all the trouble's over, and go back to being a bounty-hunter. You don't want that to happen, do you?'

11

Although he was the county sheriff and supposedly in charge of the posse deputized to fight against the outlaw gang, Luke was quite content to take a back seat to Harry. From the unassuming yet authoritative way Harry organized the defence of Mary's homestead, it was clear he had a strong military background. Why he should choose to keep the fact to himself was a mystery to Luke. However, because of the newspaper cuttings he had found in Wilson's cabin, Luke was no longer worried about his deputy's past.

Apart from Harry and Luke, the posse consisted of Jerry Grande, John and Jack Thomas, Len Williams and Sam Emmett, one of the two farmhands who had volunteered to help out on the Grande farm. Sam was no quick-draw specialist, although he always carried an old Colt, but he was a crack shot with his old Springfield musket-rifle. The other farmhand, Frank Sibley, had agreed to stay behind and guard the Grandes' farm.

Luke would have preferred to leave one, if not both, of the inexperienced Thomas brothers, instead of Sibley. However, it did mean there was an experienced war veteran guarding the Grandes' farm. Sibley was a solid, dependable man, who would not panic in the event of something going wrong.

Not that anything would go wrong, if Harry's planning and meticulous attention to detail had anything to do with it. Once the posse arrived at Mary's homestead, Luke realized the extra horses would give away their presence. He need not have worried, however, because Harry arranged for Jack to take all but Goldwind and a spare pony to the Duggans' homestead. It was just far enough away from the proposed railroad route to keep the horses safe from discovery.

Harry stationed Jerry as look-out on the ridge overlooking the homestead. Next he rigged up the water-pump so it could send a powerful jet of water over the entire roof of the homestead. Only when he considered the roof and walls of the bunkhouse too wet to burn did he permit the rest of the posse to stop pumping.

After a basic meal of beans and bacon, the rest of the posse began to make their own ammunition. As the night clouds began to cover the homestead in gloom, they heard three shots fired in quick succession. It was the prearranged signal Jerry had been instructed to give in the event of anyone approaching the homestead.

It proved to be a false alarm. It was Dr Evans in his buggy and with him was another man whom neither Luke nor Harry recognized. Apparently, the doctor had been visiting the Duggans' homestead to check one of their children, when Jack arrived with the horses. Not only had the doctor insisted on joining the posse, but so had Effram Duggan.

As Effram slowly heaved his massive frame out of the wagon, most of the posse gasped in amazement. Effram was a giant of a man, even bigger than Brad the blacksmith. His arms were thicker than most men's legs, his chest as broad as a barrel. His dark curly hair was streaked with grey, as was his bushy beard. His huge fists were almost the size of a grizzly bear's paws, an animal to which he bore more than a superficial resemblance.

Effram Duggan was, or had been, a true mountain man. Harry and Luke were happy to have this man from the wilds on their side. They were even more pleased to learn Jack had been persuaded to stay and help look after the Duggans' homestead.

'Couldn't leave my little lady and the kids on their own,' said Effram, as he winked knowingly at Luke. It seemed he had also come to the conclusion that young Jack was too likely to get in the way when the inevitable showdown came.

Dr Evans had been a surgeon during the Civil War, so he too was a more than useful addition to the posse, which now numbered seven. Hope it's a lucky number, thought Harry. He also gave thought as to how best to deploy them.

Whilst offering a good look-out position, the ridge was devoid of any cover. So although any sentry posted there would be able to raise an early warning, anyone approaching the homestead would also be able to see him. As Harry wanted to surprise the outlaw gang when they attacked, he decided to abandon the look-out on it.

Instead, he stationed Sam Emmett in the eaves of the ruined barn, where his accuracy with his Springfield would do most good. With him went John Thomas to reload, and Effram Duggan. The big mountain man had borrowed the town's double-barrelled shotgun which Harry had passed on to John.

Luke took charge of the defence of

the homestead. Supporting him was Jerry and the doctor to act as their loader. This left Harry free to scout and switch his support to wherever it was most needed when the gang attacked.

Harry was sure they would attack again. If his theory about the railroad was correct, their tracks would have to cross Mary's homestead if they were to reach Redrock. It seemed somebody wanted the property before that happened. But was it really Colonel Masters, or was he just acting on behalf of the railroad? If he was acting for the railroad, defeating him might not be enough, since the railroad could always hire someone else.

Two days passed, however, with no sign of the gang. Harry rode out to the valley where the railroad had placed its markers, only to find everything was exactly the same as when he first found them. The third, fourth and fifth days also went peacefully by. There was little for the posse to do each day but pump water on to the roof, and the ground surrounding the house and barn.

The continuous diet of bacon, beans and badly made coffee was rapidly becoming unacceptable, so Harry sent Effram hunting. The big mountain man took the doctor's buggy and drove out to the valley in which Mary had taken Harry for a picnic. Effram returned next day with the carcass of a large stag, and the news that the cattle had not been moved from the box canyon. It did not surprise anybody to learn that none of them had been rebranded.

The stag made a welcome change from beans. Effram skinned the body and cut it up as expertly as any butcher, and roasted the joints as well as any fancy restaurant chef. It lasted for three days, during which time nothing much happened. Then, just as Harry was about to give up, the gang struck.

An hour after dawn, more than twenty of them galloped down from the ridge. They made an impressive sight, but the posse was ready for them. As instructed, they held their fire until

Harry signalled.

Harry was in the corral, tending Goldwind, when he saw the outlaw gang. He raced towards the house, imitating all the signs of a man panicking at the rapid approach of so many horsemen. He ran into the house, grabbed his Henry and a box of shells, and hurried out of the back door. He waited until the half-rebuilt barn hid him from the riders, then raced across the yard to the back of the barn.

The riders opened fire, aiming at the front of the house. Harry waited until they were almost in reach of the front door before he signalled Luke to open fire. He and Jerry suddenly appeared at the windows and opened fire. Luke's Spencer carbine and Jerry's Henry rifle sent a barrage of bullets into the charging riders.

Four outlaws crashed to the ground, and at least two more were hit before the gang turned away towards the front of the barn. As they did so, Harry signalled his men in the barn to open fire. Sam's first shot struck home, then the blast from Effram's shotgun caused panic among the riders. As a man they wheeled their horses and rode blindly between the house and the barn, straight towards Harry.

He emptied his Henry into the riders as they frantically rode past. Bullets flew around him, but in their haste to escape, none of the outlaws slowed long enough to steady his aim. Unharmed, Harry dropped the empty rifle to the ground, drew his Colt and fired at the rapidly retreating outlaws until they were out of range.

Six outlaws lay dead in the yard, but three times as many had ridden away. Even if some of them were badly hurt, the posse was still outnumbered by two to one, and the element of surprise had gone. They had won the first round, but Harry was certain the outlaws would return. So far his tactics had been successful, but the outlaws would be unlikely to try a dawn attack again, nor would they be likely to risk another direct charge at the house. He guessed they would use stealth and attack under the cover of darkness. The real test was yet to come.

On the plus side, none of the posse had suffered so much as a scratch and the raid had been beaten off so quickly that only small amounts of ammunition had been used. That loss was more than offset by the five Colts and one Remington collected from the dead outlaws. Luke gave Effram the big Dragoon Colt he had taken from the sheriff's office, and picked out an Army Colt for himself. Harry selected the best out of the smaller calibre Navy Colts, while Jerry opted for the Remington New Model Army .44.

'Better than your average Colt,' said Jerry.

'I'm not so sure about that,' said Harry. 'I grant you the Remington is a mite stronger in the frame, but I prefer the Colt's balance.'

The doctor pronounced all the fallen outlaws dead. Effram and Sam were detailed to bury them. They insisted that young John came with them to help move the bodies. At first Luke disagreed, wanting to spare the boy the ordeal, but changed his mind as Sam explained.

'Most of us here have been through a bloody war, and shot enough men to haunt us for the rest of our lives. But as yet, the boy hasn't killed anyone. So let him see and smell death. Let him get the blood of the men he was willing to kill on his hands. Maybe then will he find there's little glory in killing, no honour in death. If so, he might not want to do some of the things we had to do.'

It was the longest speech Sam had ever made. To Harry and Luke, embarrassed by the all too evident signs of hero-worship they had seen in young John, it made good sense. So they agreed, and John made up the third member of the burial detail. It took almost three hours to get the job done. John's hands were still shaking as they returned, and his white face indicated he had been sick more than once. Nobody said anything when the lad refused dinner and ran quickly outside while the rest were eating.

The outlaw's gang began their second attack just before dusk. As Harry had guessed, they did not assault the house directly, but encircled it. Either the outlaws planned to starve the posse out, or they were waiting for the cover of darkness before attacking. For the moment, they formed a circle round the house and barn, thinking they were out of range. But they were wrong. Whilst they were out of range of normal rifles and Luke's Spencer carbine, the outlaw gang had not allowed for the power and accuracy of the rare Henry rifle.

The rifle-muskets most commonly used during the Civil War had been the Springfield Model 1861 and the imported British Enfield Type 1853. The Union alone had purchased over a million of them, the confederacy almost as many copies. They were all reckoned to be accurate up to 250 yards with a maximum killing range of 500 yards.

In the hands of a reasonably capable infantryman, the Henry was deadly accurate up to 1,000 yards and had a firing rate eight times faster than the Springfield, Enfield or their copies. However, officially the Confederacy had never obtained any of these magnificent rifles, whilst the Union had officially purchased a mere 1,731. Of course many more had been purchased privately, but even so, it was perhaps not so surprising the outlaws knew so little of the Henry's capabilities.

So the outlaws spread out and formed a circle, each of them some 700 yards away from the homestead buildings, well within the range of the two Henry rifles of Harry and Jerry. Of course, the single-shot carbines of the outlaws, cut-down versions of the Springfield and Enfield muzzle-loaders had not the range to reach them.

Realizing the outlaws' mistake, Harry

and Jerry left the house and walked across the yard to the corral. The two outlaws covering that side of the homestead, thinking they were out of range, stood openly and watched as Harry and the ex-mayor took aim and fired.

In spite of the distance, Harry's bullet struck the first outlaw squarely in the chest. Jerry's first missed, but the outlaw unluckily ducked into his second and died instantly.

'Too much like shooting sitting ducks,' growled Harry unhappily.

'Yes. I thought I'd done with killing, but they gave us no choice,' said Jerry, as they returned to the house.

As dusk fell, the outlaws held a council of war. It was a dark moonless night, with no hint of wind to move the cloud bank which hung oppressively over the homestead. There was nothing for the posse to do but wait for the outlaws to make their next move. Apart from Harry, who stationed himself at the back door of the house, they were all positioned as before. The hours ticked by until midnight, and then the outlaws struck again.

Under the cover of darkness, the circle of outlaws began to grow smaller as they slowly closed in on the homestead. Each outlaw carried an unlit torch made from branches cut from sagebrush, around which were wrapped strips of cut cloth soaked in lamp-oil. At a prearranged signal, the outlaws lit them, raced towards the homestead and threw the torches on to its roof.

But the lit torches revealed the outlaws' positions. Although Effram and Sam, in the barn, held their fire, a deadly hail of lead suddenly exploded from the house.

Encumbered by their lit torches, which made them easy targets, the outlaws suffered heavy casualties Three outlaws were struck down in the act of throwing their torches. As a result, their torches fell well short of their intended target and fizzled out on the wet ground, saturated by the water from the pump.

Torches thrown, the rest of the outlaws returned fire, but the flashes from the muzzle of their guns gave their positions away. With no cover to hide them, another two outlaws were fatally hit by shots from the house.

The outlaws nearest the barn broke off their attack, turned and rushed towards it. In doing so, they became silhouetted by the flames of the only torch to stay alight on the sodden roof of the house. Sam and Effram waited until the last possible moment before opening fire.

Buckshot from Effram's shotgun cut a deadly swath through the onrushing outlaws. Yet, although several outlaws fell, most made it to the barn.

By that time, the rest of the outlaws had reached the front door of the house. Alarmed by the lack of return gunfire from his friends in the front of the house, Harry ran from his position in the kitchen into the main room. He was shocked to see someone had unbolted the front door.

The outlaws came pouring through, only to be met by a fearsome volley from Luke and Jerry. They, too, had waited until the last second before firing. Harry and even the doctor joined in until they had emptied their six-guns. The room seemed full of dead or wounded outlaws, and yet still more outlaws forced their way inside, firing wildly as they did so.

The defenders discarded their empty six-guns and drew the ones taken from the outlaws killed during the first raid. Although they were far less accurate using unfamiliar pistols, their second volley was almost as deadly as the first.

Outlaws fell like ninepins. Those who were able, turned and fled. It was the outlaws' final mistake, for the defenders had emptied their guns and were helpless. Luke had correctly decided there would be too little time for the doctor to reload their guns, so had given him the last remaining Colt to increase the defenders' fire power. The strategy had worked, but it had been far too close for comfort.

The danger of being mistaken for the enemy prevented Harry from going to the barn. A bullet fired by a friend was just as likely to kill. It was possible that the barn had been overrun by the outlaws, so calling out might also prove fatal.

Moans and groans indicated that several outlaws had been wounded and were lying outside. In spite of all the dangers, and the protests of the rest of the posse, the doctor insisted on going to tend them. He was gone for about an hour before returning to say he had treated several outlaws for their wounds, then let them go on the condition they cleared out of the county and never returned.

There were, however, two seriously wounded men remaining in the yard, too badly wounded to move. The doctor had done what he could to make them comfortable, but he did not expect either to survive the night. In the event, one did. His survival was to play a significant role in the future of Redrock.

As dawn broke, the first rays of the sun shone down on the carnage in the yard. The bodies of outlaws were everywhere as Harry cautiously approached the barn. The sight which met his eyes as he entered the ruined building was almost beyond description. Blood stains were everywhere. Four outlaws lay dead, two blasted to pulp by buckshot. However, it seemed the defenders had fared little better.

Sam Emmett was dead, his body riddled with bullets; John Thomas and Effram Duggan lay unmoving on the floor. At first Harry thought they were both dead, but the big mountain man began to stir. Exhausted by the fight, and keeping guard for the rest of the night, he had merely fallen asleep. The condition of John was not so good; he was unconscious and appeared to have been shot in the ribs.

Harry called to the doctor. While he examined John and checked out the rest of the bodies, Effram explained what had happened.

'We waited for them to rush the door, then I let them have it with the shotgun. Sam was supposed to cover while I changed to the Dragoon Colt, but his gun misfired. After that, he never had a chance. Luckily for me, the other outlaws concentrated on Sam, giving me the chance to draw the Dragoon and defend myself.'

'What happened to John?' asked Harry.

'Don't rightly know. Must have caught a stray bullet.'

'Ricochet, more like,' said the doctor. 'It's smashed a rib.'

'How bad is he?' asked Jerry, who had followed the doctor into the barn.

'Lost a lot of blood, and the rib is a mess,' replied the doctor, 'but the bullet hasn't penetrated too deeply. I've seen worse recover, although I'll need to get the bullet out as soon as possible.'

Carefully, the giant Effram carried John into the kitchen and gently laid the youngster down on the table. Although John was well built for his tender years, the big mountain man handled him as easily as if he were a baby. Getting the ricocheted bullet out proved to be a tricky business, even for someone as experienced as Dr Evans, but at last he succeeded. Mercifully, John remained unconscious throughout the difficult operation, which probably aided his recovery.

While the doctor was operating, Effram held John tightly to stop the lad from moving. As there was nothing they could do to help the doctor, Harry, Luke and Jerry went outside to collect the weapons from the dead outlaws. As they did so, they discussed the situation.

'Do you think the outlaws will be back?' asked Jerry.

'Not likely. They've lost too many men,' said Luke. 'I guess the survivors will hightail it out of here.'

'No they won't,' interrupted a weak voice.

It was the only surviving outlaw. He had recovered consciousness, and although weak, was keen to repay those who had tended his wounds and kept him alive. Luke fetched some water and gave it to the wounded man.

'Easy, your fight is over,' he said to the outlaw.

'My life would be over if you hadn't looked after me,' the outlaw replied.

'Don't be too grateful. We're just saving you for the hangman's rope,' growled Jerry.

'That won't happen. They will never let me live long enough to come to trial,' said the outlaw.

'Who won't?' asked Harry.

'What's it worth to tell you?'

'Don't make deals with killers,' said Harry and Jerry simultaneously.

Luke, on the other hand, was not so sure. The man might have valuable information which could help them. He was not above letting him go free in exchange for the right kind of help. However, he could not say so in front of the other two, but he tried to give the outlaw some hope.

'No deals, but it might help if we can tell the judge you co-operated willingly.'

'It's protection I'm gonna need. Like I say, they won't let me live long enough to tell my tale in court.'

'They can't kill you if you're already dead,' said Harry.

'That's right,' continued Luke. 'Your so-called buddies left you for dead. If you help us we've no reason to tell them otherwise.'

'If you take me into town, I'm a dead man,' the outlaw's voice sunk to a whisper, his face became racked with pain.

'That's enough talking for the moment,' said Dr Evans. 'You need rest, or all my work will count for nothing.'

'Could be, under the circumstances, our prisoner might be too weak to move to town,' said Jerry.

'Could be,' agreed the doctor, catching the ex-mayor's meaning. A war-hardened surgeon, he had no scruples preventing him from manipulating the wounded man.

The tally of dead outlaws was horrific, even if they had been responsible for their own downfall. Luke finished collecting weapons and ammunition from the dead men, while Effram gently carried John to the doctor's buggy.

The doctor drove slowly into town, where John could be properly nursed. He also arranged for the undertaker to go to the homestead to collect the dead bodies. There were too many to be buried anywhere other than the town's Boot Hill.

Thanks mainly to Harry's strategy, the outlaws had been routed. Whether they had the stomach to continue fighting remained to be seen, but one thing was for sure; there would not be another attack on the homestead in the immediate future. Too many outlaws had died trying to take it, so they would have to regroup and send for reinforcements, even if the surviving outlaw was right about them not giving up.

So the decision was made to return to Jerry's farm. They had been away for far longer than they had expected, and knew the women would be worried about them. So Effram and Harry rode to the mountain man's small homestead to collect Jack and the horses.

It was clear from the run-down appearance of his homestead that Effram was no farmer. Nevertheless, his tiny wife Hannah kept their home, little more than a shack, scrupulously clean. However, it was clear the Duggans were barely eking out a living. Harry was reluctant to accept their generous hospitality and did so only to avoid giving offence.

While Effram and Paul were rounding up the horses, he suggested to Hannah that she might like to accompany her husband to the Grandes' farm. He implied Effram's services were still required on the posse, and that her presence would be most helpful in the farmhouse. None of which was strictly true, but as long as Effram remained with the posse, he would be entitled to a share of any reward collected on the dead outlaws.

So it was agreed; Hannah would pack their pitifully few belongings in their old wagon and they would drive directly to the Grande farm. In the meantime, Harry and Jack drove the posse's horses back to Mary's homestead.

The following day, the posse rode slowly back to the Grandes' farm. With them was the wounded outlaw who called himself Ned Gage. Although he had been hit by a bullet, just under his rib cage, it passed clean through him without damaging any vital organs. He had been remarkably lucky. Only a few inches higher and the bullet would have pierced his lung, just a little lower and it would have smashed into his liver.

Not that Ned felt lucky. Weak from loss of blood and pain made worse by the motion of his horse, Ned could only contemplate his doubtful future with utter dismay. The hangman's rope, or the assassin's bullet seemed to be his only options. So he was only too willing to accept the proposition put to him by Luke, when the two of them were out of earshot of the others.

12

The posse was in sombre mood as they returned to Jerry's farm. There was little elation over their victory as they all realized. The battle was far from won. Dead men could be replaced by the person or persons who had originally hired them.

Almost all of the posse had lived through the carnage of at least one bloody war. Returning to normal civilian life had been difficult for all of them, especially Luke. However, they had managed it, but now their worst nightmares had become real, and it was kill or be killed.

The women were quick to welcome them back, but equally as quick to point out that during the long time they had been away it was only too obvious that none of them had bathed. In spite of their protests, none, not even Jerry, was allowed into the farmhouse until they had showered and changed their clothes.

Although there was hot water in the house, the men were made to use cold water from the bunkhouse pump. Only the wounded raider, Ned Gage, was spared the ordeal. Half-unconscious from loss of blood and the pain from his wound, the raider was carried into the bunkhouse and laid on a bunk. In spite of the women's protests, Luke handcuffed the outlaw's right hand to the bunk rail.

The Duggans arrived before nightfall. Once again the household had to be reorganized with Harry and Luke moving into the bunkhouse, leaving their room free for Effram and his tiny wife. Standing side by side, they made an amazing sight. The huge mountain man towered over his tiny wife, who wasn't a cigar-length taller than five feet.

Harry, much to Mary's disappointment, rode off at dawn without telling her where he was going. It seemed nobody else knew Harry's plans, but Mary thought they might not be telling her to prevent her from worrying about him. Whatever the reason, their silence simply made her feel worse.

The rest of the posse spent the day supposedly doing routine tasks, tending to their horses, cleaning weapons, and making ammunition. They seemed to be taking things easy, but Mary knew better. She was the daughter of a cavalry colonel, and her husband had been an officer in the same unit, so she could read the little signs of tension she had seen in her father's regiment. The posse were preparing for a battle.

She could only guess Harry had gone scouting, as she knew he had done many times before, even if he could not remember doing so. Perhaps she had been wrong in not telling him what she knew about his past life, and the part she had played in it, but she so desperately wanted him to remember without being told.

Elizabeth was unable to read the signs and so thought that Luke was ignoring her, as she had ignored him on his last visit. Much to her annoyance, he seemed preoccupied as, indeed, did all the members of the posse, although she had no idea why.

Luke's thoughts alternated between his feelings for Elizabeth and the problems still to be overcome. After his conversations with Ned Gage, he had decided on a plan of action which he doubted would meet the approval of the rest of the posse, so kept his ideas to himself.

Harry returned later that afternoon. He had indeed been to spy out the lie of the land around the colonel's ranch. Unfortunately, the rolling prairies offered little cover, making a surprise attack out of the question.

Ever since the last raid, fragments of Harry's memory had begun to return, but they were all to do with the Civil War and completely jumbled up. As yet he could make little sense out of them, but the little of his past he could now remember filled him with disgust. At best he seemed to have been a spy; at worst, a turncoat and traitor.

After everyone had eaten, Jerry called for a meeting. Of all the members of the posse, his was the most marked change, although Mary could detect a significant change in Harry.

Jerry's confidence and self-esteem had been fully restored during the gun-battle. Gone was the diffidence, the hesitation and the servile attitude he had previously adopted in the presence of Colonel Masters. The six-gun he now wore constantly ensured no one would ever push him around again.

In spite of their protests, this time Mrs Grande and the rest of the women were excluded from the meeting. When it was over, the men would not discuss what they had decided to do, feeling the less the womenfolk knew about the dangerous course of action they were about to undertake, the better.

Of course, the posse was wrong.

Exclusion from the discussions only confirmed Mrs Grande's suspicions that Jerry was planning to do something reckless. It did not take her long to wheedle it out of Jerry as soon as the meeting was over, and she lost no time in telling her daughter and Mary.

Knowing Harry the way she did, Mary was not surprised to learn he had devised the plan. Elizabeth was both alarmed and furious when she heard that Luke's part was to be the most dangerous. She stormed out of the house and found him alone in the corral, grooming Josh.

'Attacking Colonel Master's ranch is crazy. You will all get yourselves killed,' she said angrily.

'What's the alternative?' said Luke. 'If we do nothing, he will simply recruit more outlaws, and the raids will start all over again.'

'You don't know for certain the colonel's behind the raids,' said Elizabeth.

'We do. We have a witness, even if he

won't testify in court.'

'So you're going to take the law into your own hands,' snapped Elizabeth.

'I am the law,' said Luke calmly.

'But he has a ranch full of gun-hands. You will all be killed!'

'Your father can look after himself. As for me, this is how I earn my living. When it's all over here, there will be another man like Colonel Masters to fight, or another wanted man to track down. Look, Elizabeth, I'm a bounty-hunter. That's why your father summoned me to Redrock.'

'You could stay here when it's all over if you wanted to,' said Elizabeth.

Luke was taken by surprise, but before he could find out what she meant, Harry interrupted them. He had decided to groom Goldwind after his long ride. Feeling she had said too much, Elizabeth took advantage of the interruption and rushed back into the house, leaving Luke totally bemused.

Next morning the posse left for the colonel's ranch. This time they left young Jack Thomas behind. After the injury sustained by his elder brother, Mr Grande waved aside all his protests. So, in order to lessen the blow to the boy's pride, he was given the job of guarding Ned Gage. However, weakened by the loss of blood and handicapped by his wounds, there was little chance of the outlaw escaping.

Frank Sibley joined the posse, coldly determined to avenge the death of his friend Sam Emmett. In his present mood, Frank was worth three or four hired gunmen.

Much to Elizabeth's surprise, Effram was not riding on one of the spare horses her father owned, but drove his old wagon. Neither she nor her mother could understand why, but Mary knew. Even though she was well aware of the danger he and the rest of the posse faced, she could not help smiling. It was a tactic her father had used several times during the Civil War and the thought that Harry was going to use it now gave her immense pleasure.

Slowed down by Effram's old wagon, the posse travelled all day and camped that night. They started up an hour before dawn and arrived at the colonel's ranch at daybreak to find little sign of activity.

No guards had been posted, and the approach of one old wagon caused little interest until its driver was recognized as Luke Donovan. On his lap was his Spencer carbine.

As the wagon pulled into the yard, the so-called ranch hands began to gather round it. Luke noticed some of them moved with some difficulty. Clearly they were carrying wounds, further proof to Luke of the involvement of the colonel in the raid on Mary's homestead.

Luke pulled up the wagon beside the ranch-house door and called out.

'Masters, I want a word with you.'

As he did so, the ranch hands noticed Luke was still wearing his badge of office, something the colonel remarked upon as he stepped into the yard. He

252

appeared to be unarmed.

'Well, Mr Donovan, what do you want? I'm not used to callers at this time of day.'

'You're under arrest,' said Luke calmly.

'Apart from the fact that you have been stripped of office and I have issued a warrant for your arrest for the murder of Zack Blake, what makes you think you can take me in?'

'My appointment is from the county, not your town. In any case, you're a wanted war criminal. You rode with Quantrill.'

'So what are you going to do about it?' laughed the colonel.

'Shoot you, if necessary. Dead or alive, you're coming with me and my men. Frankly, I prefer dead. It makes it easier to collect the reward money.'

As he spoke the sides of the covered wagon were flung open to reveal Effram and Frank Sibley. Both aimed their old Springfield rifles at the ranch hands, but, while they held the advantage, they could not hope to outgun all the ranch hands.

'Shoot them, you fools,' snapped the colonel, 'there's only three of them.'

At that moment Harry and Jerry rode out from behind the colonel's barn and dismounted. The ranch hands had been too engrossed in the goings-on in the yard to notice the two other members of the posse as they circled behind the big barn.

Unlike the Fosters' ruined barn, the colonel's barn was an imposing structure, situated several hundred yards from the main house. As such, it was well beyond the accurate killing range of either the Springfield and Enfield rifles used by the ranch hands. However, the distance was no problem for the two Henry rifles now aimed at them by Harry and Jerry.

'Well, go on, kill them,' shrieked the colonel.

The ranch hands tensed and Luke's right hand dived towards his Colt. Silently, he cursed himself for staying on the wagon. The high position made him a sitting duck.

Suddenly one of the hands, presumably their leader, threw his gun-hand up in the air and yelled out.

'Hold on, now, let's not be too hasty, Sheriff. Let's talk some more. Tell your men to back off and I'll tell mine to do the same.'

'Agreed,' said Luke, moving his right hand away from his Colt and motioning to Harry not to fire.

'Just now you said our colonel had ridden for Quantrill. That true?' asked the leading ranch hand.

'What if it is? I've paid you good money to carry out my orders,' said the colonel.

'True,' said the ranch hand, 'but most of us here fought in the war. Maybe we ain't much, but I for one ain't going to work for no Quantrill man after what he and his men did.'

'Fools! I'll double your pay if you kill them,' shouted the colonel.

'Not me,' said one of the ranch

hands. 'I fought for the Confederacy and proud of it. Came home though to find my kinfolk had been killed in one of Quantrill's raids.'

'I sure as hell ain't going to go up against two Henry rifles again, not for no man, Quantrill's man or not,' said one of the wounded ranch hands.

There was a chorus of agreeing voices from the rest of the ranch hands. The colonel went to turn back into his house but found his way blocked by Frank Sibley.

'Just give me the excuse to shoot, that's all I ask,' he said, pointing his old rifle at the colonel.

But he didn't get the chance. Throwing caution to the wind, Effram dropped his rifle and struck the colonel. The mountain man's huge fist connected squarely with the colonel's jaw and he went down as if he was pole-axed.

'Well, Sheriff, I guess that leaves us with just one problem,' said the leading ranch hand ominously.

'What's that?' asked Luke.

'Me and the boys are going to collect our gear and the money due to us, then we aim to ride out of here. What are you going to do about it?'

'Nothing, provided you give me your word you will keep on going and never come back,' replied Luke.

'You got it, Sheriff, ain't he boys?' replied the leading ranch hand.

An hour later, all the ranch hands left. As deputy, Harry was chosen to escort them to the county line. Like Luke, he was only too aware that some of the ranch hands were the outlaws who had raided Mary's homestead and that others had been part of other raids. Nevertheless, he agreed with Luke's decision to let them go. There had been too much bloodshed already.

It was a jubilant homecoming. The posse's journey home was delayed by Effram's old wagon, so Harry caught up with them before they reached Jerry's farm.

When the women saw the captured colonel, they realized the fighting was over and their men had returned unharmed. Mrs Grande flung her arms round her husband, and Effram lifted his tiny wife off the ground as she tried to kiss him. To his surprise, Mary flung her arms around Harry as soon as he dismounted and kissed him passionately. Luke went immediately to see the prisoner they had left in the care of young Paul, giving Elizabeth no chance to show her feelings.

After making the same promise as the rest of the so-called ranch hands, Ned Gage was released and rode slowly away, complaining his wounds were still troubling him. The colonel was manacled to the same bunk Ned had been handcuffed to, and the posse took it in turns to stand guard over him.

After dinner that night, Frank Sibley took his turn to guard the colonel, while the others sat in the dining room discussing the events of the last few days. Jerry and his wife sat arm in arm on the sofa, while Hannah Duggan perched herself on her husband's massive knees. Mary was no less familiar, cuddling into Harry as they squeezed closely together on one large easy-chair. Elizabeth was a little too uncertain of Luke's feelings to be quite so familiar, so she contented herself with sitting next to him, and squeezing his hand when she thought nobody was looking. However, Mrs Grande noticed and smiled approvingly.

'Luke, how did you know the colonel had ridden with Quantrill?' asked Jerry. 'After all, he came to Redrock well before the end of the war.'

'And why didn't you let us in on the secret?' asked Harry.

'Well, Harry, at first I thought you might be the man,' said Luke apologetically. 'Then when I found those newspaper cuttings in Wilson's cabin, I thought Burt must be the man I was looking for.'

'I guess I thought that, but with so much else going on I never got round to telling you folks. As it turned out, maybe that was just as well,' said Jerry ruefully.

'But you still haven't explained how you knew about the colonel,' said Elizabeth.

'During our ride back from Mary's place I got talking with Ned Gage. He told me Burt Wilson and the colonel knew each other from the war.'

'Are you saying Wilson rode with Quantrill after all?' asked Jerry.

'No. From what Ned said. Wilson worked for a railroad.'

'The Western Central,' said Harry.

'Yes,' replied Luke, 'but even then I didn't make the connection between him and the colonel.'

'Well, if Ned was still working for the railroad, perhaps he tipped off the colonel they were planning a line to Redrock . . . ' said Harry.

'That's what I thought,' said Luke. 'Then I got to thinking why had Wilson kept those old newspaper clippings about Quantrill? Then it dawned on me. Wilson wasn't just tipping off the colonel about the forthcoming railway; he was blackmailing him.'

'And that's why he kept the clippings,' said Mary.

'Well, my guess is that Wilson kept those handy to keep the colonel in line,' said Luke. 'In themselves, they only give clues to the colonel's past. But I'm betting Wilson has some more stashed safely away that connect the colonel to Quantrill.'

Suddenly two shots rang out from the bunkhouse, followed by a third. Unencumbered by the close attentions of a partner, Luke was first to the scene. He found Paul badly wounded, and Frank Sibley lying dead in a pool of blood by the bunk to which the colonel had been chained. The chain had been severed by a bullet, and the colonel had disappeared.

The sound of horses' hoofs galloping away told their own story. Harry, closely followed by the rest, came racing up. He took one look at the body and ushered the women out of the bunkhouse.

Cursing under his breath at his own stupidity, Luke saddled Josh and rode out into the night. There was no chance of tracking the colonel and his rescuers, but he did not have to, since he knew there was only one place for the colonel to go.

Mary, no stranger to the sight of dead or dying men, refused to go. She tried to make young Paul as comfortable as possible, but she knew there was nothing anyone could do.

'It was Ned Gage. Came back saying he had forgotten to tell us something important, but could we help him to a bunk as his wound was hurting him. While we had our backs turned, someone else must have sneaked in. There was a shot and Frank fell. I tried to tell them I didn't have a gun, but Ned just picked up Frank's and shot me.'

'Quiet,' whispered Mary. 'Rest easy. Luke's already gone for the doctor.'

But Paul could not hear her. He had lapsed into unconsciousness from which he was destined never to recover. Grim-faced, Harry returned to the house. Nobody had to ask him how Jack was, nor why he filled his canteen.

White-faced, Mary returned to the house. Without a word, she packed some food for Harry while Mrs Grande consoled her daughter. Effram's wife Hannah made coffee for all of them.

Effram was delegated to guard the farm. At first light Harry saddled up Goldwind and Jerry his pony. The ground was still soft, so Harry had no difficulty picking up the tracks left by the colonel and his rescuers. He also noticed a separate fourth set of tracks which he recognized as belonging to Josh.

At first, all the tracks led towards town, but then one split away. Harry noticed the tracks of Josh followed those which headed into town. As Jerry's pony could not match Goldwind in speed or stamina, Jerry followed the tracks leading to town while Harry rode after the other set of tracks, hoping Ned Gage was riding the horse.

Goldwind almost flew over the ground, but Harry soon reined him in. He did not want to exhaust his steed, merely to wind him. He walked Goldwind until the horse had recovered, then set off at a steady trot. Now Goldwind would be able to go on for two or even three hours before the stallion would have to rest.

It was an old Indian trick he remembered from his childhood. It was also the first time he had remembered anything about his life before the Civil War. He brushed the memory to one side. It had been a long time since he had acted as a scout, so he needed all his concentration to follow the trail.

An hour later the tracks changed significantly. The stride became much shorter, which meant the horse Harry was following was blown. Unlike Harry, its rider had pushed his mount too hard without giving it time to recover. Harry smiled, but there was no joy in his eyes, just cold hate. Goldwind was still full of running, so there was every chance he would catch up with the rider, even though he was several hours ahead of him.

13

It was still dark when Luke rode into Redrock. The saloon was still lit up, but there was little sound of activity coming from its interior. However, two hot and sweating horses loosely tethered outside it told Luke he would find his quarry inside.

Apart from two sleepy-eyed saloon girls and the barkeeper, the saloon appeared empty. The barkeeper seemed friendly enough, but the sudden look of apprehension in one of the girls' eyes told Luke he had walked into a trap.

'We're just closing up, Sheriff, but there's always the private bottle for friends,' said the barkeeper.

'No thanks, I'm looking for the colonel or Burt Wilson,' replied Luke.

'Haven't seen the colonel in a couple of days,' said the barkeeper. 'As for Burt, he's the town's new sheriff, but you've just missed him. He's been here all night. Ain't that right, girls?'

Both nodded their heads in eager agreement, but Luke thought he saw a warning look in one of the girls' eyes as she glanced towards the bar doors.

'I guess he will go back to your old office before going on patrol. Go out the back way. If you hurry, you might catch him.'

The call girl's head shook fractionally, just enough for Luke to see. He drew his Colt.

'You seem just a mite too eager for me to go back outside, friend,' he said.

'Just trying to be helpful, Sheriff.'

Using his left hand, Luke removed his hat. Then with the help of the saloon girl who had tried to warn him, eased off his coat.

'Put them on,' he ordered the barkeeper.

'There's no need for all this fuss,' protested the barkeeper, but he did as he was told.

'Now suppose you go out through

the back door,' said Luke.

The barkeeper's face turned white as a look of horror shot across his face.

'No!' he gasped. 'Not dressed like this.'

Luke cocked his Colt and pointed it in the direction of the bar doors. The barkeeper shuffled from behind the bar and made his way slowly towards the door. He began to plead with Luke.

'For pity's sake, don't make me go out there dressed like this. You don't understand.'

'I understand you wanted me to go back outside, so take your choice. Step outside and take a chance on your friends, or I will shoot you for certain.'

'You're a lawman. You wouldn't shoot me.'

'Not really. I'm a bounty-hunter, and there's a price on the colonel's head. But this is personal. Your boss killed young Paul Thomas when he escaped. An unarmed kid who had never harmed anyone. Shot him down without a chance. So anyone who sides with the colonel will have to answer to me. So don't kid yourself, if you're not out of the saloon pronto, you're a dead man.'

'They will kill me,' whispered the bartender.

'Probably. But I'm a fair man. Call out to your friends and tell them it's not me. There's only a slim chance they won't shoot but that's more than young Paul had.'

The cold look of death in Luke's eyes convinced the barkeeper his only chance was to go outside. He called to the waiting gunmen as he ran through the doors, but to no avail. They opened fire from the other side of the still dark street, and the barkeeper slumped to the ground, his body riddled by bullets.

It was almost the last thing the gunmen did, however. Thinking they had killed Luke, they moved from the safety of their hiding places and walked over to the body. Too late, they discovered it was not Luke. He stepped into the street and emptied his six-gun into them.

The first gunman was slammed back into the alleyway in which he had been hiding by the impact of the bullets. The second gunman staggered forward across the street. As he fell to his knees, a look of disbelief was etched into his face. He looked up at Luke and stretched out his hands towards him, as if begging him to stop the blood pouring from his chest. He tried to speak, but blood gurgled from his mouth as he slithered to the ground. So died Burt Wilson.

Too late, Luke heard the laugh behind him. He threw down his empty six-gun then turned, drew, cocked and fired his spare Colt. As he did so, the world about him exploded in a blinding flash of agony. Then black nothingness descended in a cloak all around him, and he fell to the ground.

Derringer in hand, Colonel Masters stood, staring wide-eyed at the fallen lawman, the look of satisfaction frozen on his face. Luke's bullet had struck him right between the eyes.

14

Even if he had known about the shootings in town, Ned would not have cared. He had troubles of his own. In his panic to put as much distance between himself and the Grandes' spread, he had flogged his horse to death.

So now he was on foot. Not daring to go back he walked on, always looking out for a lone rider. His plan was simple; one shot from his trusty Springfield would down the rider before he could get within pistol-shot, then he would take the dead man's horse and ride on to the next town, steal another horse and ride on again. A simple, effective plan, but with one flaw; he walked for hours without seeing another rider.

Panic-stricken, Ned had no thought to cover his tracks, even when he was on foot. Harry passed the dead horse and had little difficulty in following Ned until he came to a sharp ridge. It was a hard climb so once they had reached the top, he dismounted and poured the last of his water into his upturned hat. Goldwind drank gratefully. Harry remounted and rode along the ridge crest until he saw a movement way below him, but the man was too far away for him to be certain it was Ned Gage.

Harry reached for his field-glasses. Of course they were not there. For a moment he had thought he was back in the Civil War, scouting ahead of his troopers. Unbidden, visions of his men came flooding back, only to be chased away by a bullet thudding into the ground some way below him.

If Harry had not recognized Ned, the outlaw recognized Harry, seated as he was on the magnificent Goldwind. Stationary on the top of the ridge, Harry made a good target. Ned's trusty Springfield was already loaded, so the outlaw took careful aim and fired.

To Ned's dismay, the bullet fell well short. The Springfield was a single-shot muzzle-loader, so the outlaw desperately began to reload. That took even an experienced infantryman about twenty seconds, but Ned was hot, tired and scared and fumbled badly.

While Ned was desperately reloading, Harry dismounted and slid the Henry from its resting place behind his saddle. The long barrel of the repeating rifle made it a cumbersome weapon for horseback use, but as an infantry weapon, it still had no rival.

Harry took careful aim and fired, but the bullet passed harmlessly over the head of his adversary. He had not allowed sufficiently for the height of the ridge.

How often he had lectured his troopers about making the same mistake. Where were they now? Unbidden, the memories came flooding back, but he turned them aside. Now was not the time.

Ned fired again, but although he had adjusted for the height of the ridge, the bullet still fell short. Desperately the outlaw began to reload, but he only just finished priming the Springfield when Harry fired again. This time he did not miss. Ned fell to the ground as if pole-axed, never to rise again.

Harry relaxed, a grim smile of satisfaction spread across his face. The murder of young Paul had been avenged. He returned the Henry to its resting place, remounted Goldwind and headed home as quickly as possible. There was much work still to be done.

However, with so many bodies to bury, the busiest man in Redrock was the undertaker. There was little time for formality, but the man did his best to ensure the outlaws had a decent burial. Each grave had at least a wooden marker bearing the name of its occupant. One such marker was a little more elaborate, bearing the name Luke Donovan. Yet the body was buried with no more ceremony than those of the outlaws, and no one came to visit the grave.

After the burials, Redrock returned to its former quiet self. Jerry Grande, once again the town mayor, formally announced that the railroad would not now be coming to Redrock. The activities of the Western Central were to be investigated by the Federal authorities and those responsible for running it had been arrested.

The town's quiet routine was only slightly interrupted by the disappearance of Luke's horse, Josh. The incident occurred the day following the payout of the reward money offered for Masters and several of the dead outlaws.

That same day, Elizabeth left on the stage to take an extended holiday with an aunt, who, it was said, lived in one of the southern states. Rumour was it was Virginia but the Grandes were strangely evasive about the affair. Indeed, nobody in Redrock had ever heard any of the Grande family mention they had relatives in the south.

Masters had never been a real colonel, but had ridden with Quantrill who had given him the title for his part in some of the bloodiest and worst atrocities committed during the Civil War. The reward money for him and some of the other outlaws killed at his ranch was substantial, and with his share Effram bought the Grandes' farm for his wife. With the money left over, he was able to hire hands to do most of the farm work while he went into his beloved mountains to hunt.

With their share of the reward money, the proceeds from the sale of their farm and a sizeable mortgage from the bank. Jerry Grande purchased Colonel Masters' ranch. He took to the life as if born to it, and headed the drive of the supposedly rustled herd to Dodge. Beef prices were good that year; the money he obtained for the herd set the Grandes up for the rest of their lives.

Harry gave most of his reward money

to Mary, then helped Jerry drive his herd to Dodge. While he was away, Mary used part of the money to pay off her debt and used the rest to buy Effram's old spread. On its own, Effram's spread was worthless, but it was the next property to Mary's homestead. By buying it Mary also acquired the land in between the two properties, so increasing the size of her land fourfold.

By the time he returned from Dodge, Harry's memory had almost fully returned. He remembered why he came to Redrock and sorted out his life during the Civil War. Although there were still important parts of his life which were still blank, at least he knew who and what he had been. Yet there were still questions to which he had no answers. The most important of which concerned Mary, so at the first opportunity he began to question her.

She did not answer but suggested another picnic. This time they walked to the secluded spot at the back of the homestead, and stopped near an unmarked grave. Over the picnic lunch, Harry began to tell Mary what he now remembered about his past.

He had been born in Texas. His father had been killed during the Texas — Mexico War. He had no recollection of his mother at all, but remembered being brought up at the monastery at Paulo Marino where he had received a good education. At sixteen he had left the monastery and gone to San Antonio to seek his fortune as a cowboy. He was soon taken on, although at first he had to settle for being a wrangler at seventy-five cents a day.

Until the outbreak of the Civil War, he had ridden the Shawnee Trail, driving one big herd after another from the heart of Texas, a thousand or more miles across the Indian Territories, then through Kansas right into St Louis.

He remembered that it was not hostile Indians that were the main problem they had to contend with, but Kansas farmers. It was those same farmers who finally succeeded in closing the trail to St Louis.

The outbreak of the Civil War found him stranded in St Louis and like thousands of others, he joined the Confederate Army. At the time he had believed the war was about the right of the Southern states to withdraw from the United States, and determine their own future. Events were to change his mind.

At first, however, all went well. Except his horse was taken for use by the cavalry and he found himself in the infantry. He fought at both the Battles of Bull Run and was made up to corporal. However, after the South's initial success, things started to go badly wrong.

General Lee may have been a brilliant tactician, but he did not seem to understand the needs of a large army. While some of Lee's senior officers rode around in splendid uniforms, most of the Confederate rank and file were reduced to rags and went barefooted. Provisions for food seemed as non-existent as the pay.

After much hardship the final straw came when a mounted officer ordered him to give up his Colt Dragoon pistol. As it was the only thing he possessed which had belonged to his father, he refused. Found guilty of insubordination, he was sentenced to be flogged like a slave.

Thanks to an understanding junior officer tasked to oversee the punishment, the actual flogging had been reduced to a minimum, but he had been stripped of his rank and made to dig latrines, existing on water and a little stale bread.

He lost not only his Dragoon Colt, but they had also taken his musket and what little money he had managed to save. He remembered how the injustice of his treatment had made him question his loyalty to the Confederacy. After all he was a Texan, first and foremost.

Although Texas was a slave state, he had ridden with many Negroes along the Shawnee trail and found them little different from himself. He began to realize they had been the lucky few and his unjust treatment had made him realize that slavery was wrong.

He was then assigned to an advance unit and ordered to dig new latrines. The site was near a wood some distance from the camp. While he was away digging, the camp was raided by Union cavalry.

Armed only with a spade, Harry remembered the exact moment he decided against fighting. For the only time in his life, he took cover, returning to the camp after the shooting had stopped. What was left of his camp was in absolute chaos. However, the Union attack had been rebuffed, their troops receiving a heavy mauling in the process. His own unit had pulled out, presumably assuming he had been killed.

He remembered the scene of carnage as if it were only yesterday. Dead bodies lay all around, mostly Union cavalry men. Then came the rain, as heavy as any he had ever encountered. His own clothes were in tatters and he had no boots. So reluctantly he searched amongst the dead bodies until he came across a young officer of similar height and build to himself. Soaking wet and shivering with cold, he took the dead man's jacket, neither a grey Confederate nor a blue Union tunic, but a non-standard buckskin.

In one of the coat pockets he found a letter and written orders. The dead officer was a scout who had been on his way to join a crack Union cavalry unit. Why the scout had involved himself in this particular skirmish, Harry never found out, but in taking the unfortunate officer's coat, Harry unwittingly changed the rest of his life.

From another corpse Harry took a Navy Colt and from another a pair of boots that fitted him. In the appalling conditions created by the deluge, to a man who had no boots, it mattered little they were dead men's boots, or that the man he was taking them from had been a Union officer.

A fly settled momentarily on his face, bringing Harry back to the present. Mary passed him a sandwich which he began to eat. Then he paused as he remembered how much he had hated scavenging among the rest of the corpses for food and ammunition. His success in scavenging had almost been his undoing. Forgetting he was clad in Union clothes, he made his way back to Confederate lines, only to be shot by a jumpy sentry. When he came round, he was in a field hospital, but it had belonged to the Union, not the Confederacy.

He still remembered his feeling of astonishment when he discovered he was not a prisoner but a patient. He had been mistaken for the dead scout. After he recovered, there had been little alternative but to continue the imper-sonation, otherwise he would have been shot as a spy.

So he played the role of the

buckskin-clad scout for the rest of the war. However, this was not without the connivance of his commanding officer. Even at the height of the Civil War the Union Army kept good records, especially of the officers who had trained at West Point.

When the dead man's records finally caught up with him, they only served to confirm the suspicions of Harry's commanding officer. He had already guessed that Harry was an impostor. By then, however, Harry had already struck up a very close relationship with the CO's daughter.

Harry's ability was such he had become the unit's chief scout and there was no doubt in the CO's mind as to Harry's loyalty to the Union, so he did nothing and told nobody, not even when Harry asked permission to marry his daughter.

A month after they married, Harry's CO, now his father-in-law, had been killed in action. A few weeks before the end of the war, Harry had been tasked to scout around Redrock. He had adopted the role of a drunk to enable him to spy on the town. Finding it was no longer occupied by Confederate troops, he returned to his unit. Leading them back to town, he was blown up as they charged across a bridge.

Harry remembered nothing after the explosion until he found himself sweeping the saloon back in Redrock. But he now realized two people must have known who he was all the time. One was Dr Evans, and the other, of course, was Mary.

'Why have you never said anything to me?' he asked her.

'We knew you had scouted Redrock, so I persuaded Dr Evans to come and look for you. He found you and told me of the state you were in. As soon as the war ended, I came to Redrock and bought the homestead with the money Dad left me. Redrock didn't have a doctor at the time, so it seemed only natural for Doctor Evans to stay on.'

'That still doesn't explain why you

didn't tell me, when I came to my senses,' said Harry.

'But you hadn't. Yes, you had stopped being the drunken bum the townsfolk called the Barfly, but you had enough problems without me adding to them.'

'Well, they're over now and I have most of my memory back. I'm ready to begin again if you are.'

'Of course, my dear.'

Mary stood up and took Harry by the hand and led him to the unmarked grave. They stood in silent respect for a few moments before Harry spoke.

'We must mark the grave properly,' he said. 'Your father was a fine man, and the best commanding officer I ever served with.'

Hand in hand, they walked back to the house. Mary smiled contentedly, although she was unable to keep back her tears of happiness. Finally, her Harry had come back to her.

'Welcome home, husband,' she said, as she closed the door behind them.

We do hope that you have enjoyed reading this large print book.

Did you know that all of our titles are available for purchase?

We publish a wide range of high quality large print books including:
Romances, Mysteries, Classics
General Fiction
Non Fiction and Westerns

Special interest titles available in large print are:
The Little Oxford Dictionary
Music Book, Song Book
Hymn Book, Service Book

Also available from us courtesy of Oxford University Press:
Young Readers' Dictionary
(large print edition)
Young Readers' Thesaurus
(large print edition)

For further information or a free brochure, please contact us at:
Ulverscroft Large Print Books Ltd.,
The Green, Bradgate Road, Anstey,
Leicester, LE7 7FU, England.
Tel: (00 44) **0116 236 4325**
Fax: (00 44) **0116 234 0205**

THE CHISELLER

Tex Larrigan

Soon the paddle steamer would be on its long journey down the Missouri River to St Louis. Now, all Saul Rhymer had to do was to play the last master stroke of the evening. He looked at the mounting pile of gold and dollar bills and again at the cards in his hand. Then, looking around the table, he produced the deed to the goldmine in Montana. 'Let's play poker!' But little did he know how that journey back to St Louis would change his life so drastically.

THE ARIZONA KID

Andrew McBride

When former hired gun Calvin Taylor took the job of sheriff of Oxford County, New Mexico, it was for one reason only — to catch, or kill, the notorious Arizona Kid, and pick up the fifteen hundred dollars reward the governor had secretly offered. Taylor found himself on the trail of the infamous gang known as the Regulators, hunting down a man who'd once been his friend. The pursuit became, in every sense, a journey of death.

BULLETS IN BUZZARDS CREEK

Bret Rey

The discovery of a dead saloon girl is only the beginning of Sheriff Jeff Gilpin's problems. Fortunately, his old friend 'Doc' Holliday arrives in Buzzards Creek just as Gilpin is faced by an outlaw gang. In a dramatic shoot-out the sheriff kills their leader and Holliday's reputation scares the hell out of the others. But it isn't long before the outlaws return, when they know Holliday is not around, and Gilpin is alone against six men . . .